SECRET OF THE Viking Dagger

TIME WARP BOOK

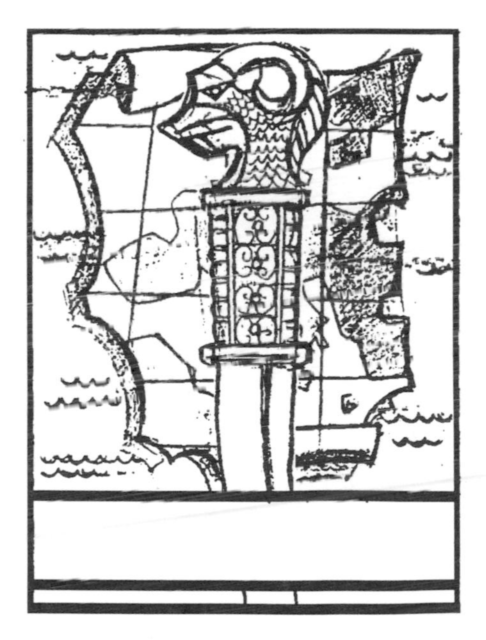

To Lucy,
Enjoy this Viking tale!

SECRET OF THE Viking Dagger

SCARLETT
RYAN FOSTER

North Sea Press • Fiction Division
SAN ANTONIO, TEXAS

SECRET OF THE Viking Dagger

SCARLETT
RYAN FOSTER

Editor: James Qualben, Ph.D.
Cover and Text Illustrations: Aundrea Hernandez
Dagger Art: Edgar Duncan, Jr.
Cover Graphics: Michael Qualben

First Printing 1997
Printed in the United States of America

Published by LANGMARC PUBLISHING
North Sea Press • Fiction Division
P.O. 33817 • San Antonio, TX 78265
1-800-864-1648

Library of Congress Cataloging-in-Publication Data
Foster, Scarlett Ryan, 1961-
Secret of the Viking Dagger / Scarlett Ryan Foster.
p. cm.
Includes bibliographical references (p. 136)
Summary: Two young brothers discover a buried Viking dagger near their Michigan home and find themselves transported to tenth-century Norway, where they are forced to accompany Viking warriors as they search for their kidnapped children across Europe and into Africa.
ISBN 1-880292-55-6 (pbk.: alk paper). --ISBN 1-880292-56-4 (lib. hardcover : alk. paper)
[1. Vikings--Fiction. 2. Time travel--Fiction. 3. Brothers--Fiction.] I. Title.
PZ7.F8165Se 1997
[Fic]--dc21 96-51184
CIP

Dedication

To my husband, Ben, and our families—
the Ryans and Fosters—
for all their encouragement and support.

CONTENTS

1

Discovery

"Look at this, Dave," Ben shouted. He ran toward his younger brother who waited on his trail bike. Ben held a long piece of machinery. David laughed as he watched Ben struggle to carry it.

"What is that thing?" David asked.

"Grandpa said we could use it today. It's a metal detector. He showed me how it works. Let's go to the woods and look for lost treasure," Ben said.

"Is this what he uses to find all those old coins and stuff along the beach?"

"Yeah. Hurry up! Let's go find some treasure," Ben said. "I get to use it first."

After a few minutes of waving the detector over dead leaves and twigs, Ben felt a tug on his shirt sleeve. "It's my turn now. You've had it for fifteen minutes and all you've found are a couple of rusty nails."

"All right! If you're so sure we're actually going to find something, help yourself."

David grabbed the detector and left the ancient Indian trail. They walked deeper into the woods.

The brothers explored for a long time and decided to return to their bikes if they didn't find any treasure in the next ten minutes. David was the "last man," so his job was to look behind them every few minutes. He made a mental picture of the landmarks they passed so they wouldn't get lost. When the woods grew thick, he snapped off twigs for markers.

Suddenly, the metal detector made loud clicking sounds. Ben was behind the trunk of a huge old oak tree. Its canopy of broad green leaves reflected a hazy green light on everything below. David rushed over to see what was going on. Had they located buried pirate treasure? Better yet, the remains of space aliens? Suddenly Ben screamed.

"What is it?" David shouted.

"The handle is so hot I can hardly hold on. It is shaking like it wants me to let go." Ben was struggling. "Help me hang on. I think we've found something!"

David reached lower on the handle and held on with both hands. "Maybe it's getting overheated," he shouted. The racket was so loud the boys couldn't hear each other. The rapid clicking sound changed to a screech.

As if it had been struck by lightning, the metal detector bolted from their hands. Both boys were tossed around like leaves in a storm. Then the chaos stopped. There was an eerie silence. No birds, no squirrels, no insects—not even the sound of the boys' breathing. The boys were too frightened to move. Ben glanced at David whose eyes looked like saucers. They both trembled as they cautiously stood up.

The boys brushed off their clothes and felt for broken bones. They found only a few bruises. Returning to school with an arm or leg in a cast would have made their story more convincing.

They gawked at the metal detector and then at the spot where they had been seconds before. Nothing seemed unusual—no giant bean stalk or anything. It was like waking up from a nightmare. Ben spoke first, a bit frightened by the sound of his own voice. "Let's dig around here and forget the metal detector."

"Good idea," David whispered. "Hey, do you think we wandered onto some ancient burial ground or something?"

"How would I know?" Ben was regaining his confidence. The boys walked to the spot where it all started. They knelt on the ground and carefully removed vines and a few wild mint plants. They found nothing but forest dirt and scattered old pine needles. Ben picked up a thick stick and David removed a small beach shovel from his backpack.

The brothers decided it couldn't have been lightning, because nothing was burned or smelled toasted. Even their clothes and hair were all right, although they were dirty from being thrown around the forest floor.

They were ready to give up their digging when Ben noticed something small, flat, and round that reflected a glint of light. "Wow, look," he cried out. "This may be something."

David wore a disgusted frown when he looked at the piece of metal between Ben's fingers. Slightly annoyed, he asked, "That's what tore the detector from our hands?" Ben wiped the object on his T-shirt.

"Hey, it's a coin, and it looks really old," Ben said. His fear of the unexplained event was evaporating.

"It's got some funny letters or something on it," David said as he examined it. "Is it an Indian coin?"

"Indians didn't have coins, stupid. Mom will probably know what it is or at least where we can learn about it."

The boys looked at the metal detector lying at the base of the oak tree. David waggled his finger at Ben and said, "Don't even think about it! We'd better not use that thing until we find out what's wrong with it." Ben was secretly relieved as they resumed digging. He tucked the strange coin in the front pocket of his jeans.

The boys were shoveling dirt with their crude tools when David's beach shovel hit something hard. Thud! David and Ben dropped their makeshift tools and started digging with their bare hands so they wouldn't ruin anything valuable. David screamed with delight as his hands found the edge of some type of metal box. "Knowing our luck, it'll turn out to be an old tool box," Ben muttered.

"Just keep digging. Why would anyone bury an old tool box way out here?" David was excited. They found another edge and another. Finally, the last pointed edge was exposed and the boys stared at the top of a box the size of a large trunk. There was no way of knowing how deep it was.

The boys lost track of time as they worked to unearth their treasure. They needed better tools. They decided to return to the cabin for shovels, a rope, and a pulley. Besides, they were getting hungry. Ben also wanted to ask their mother about the coin. David and Ben promised each other that they would not tell anyone what else they had found—not yet anyway.

When they arrived at the cabin, it was well past lunch time and their grandfather was worried about them. The boys were so excited that they ran right past the table of sandwiches and lemonade. They headed straight to their mother's office where she did much of her historical research and writing. "Mom! Mom! Look what David and I found in the woods!" Ben shouted as he burst through the doorway.

Mrs. Ryan looked up from her papers. Ben thrust the coin into her palm. David blurted, "What is it? Where did it come from? What do the letters mean?"

"Well, let me clean it off, and we'll have a look at it under the magnifier lens," Mrs. Ryan said. Her soft voice reflected her habit of working in libraries and museums. She studied the coin for a long time. She walked to a shelf and brought two books back to her work table. One was about Vikings and the other about Arabic archeology. The boys were impatient. They knew their discovery must be something important or their mother wouldn't proceed with such caution.

"Are you boys sure you found this in the woods?" They nodded enthusiastically. "You just may have found something very special. Look here." Mrs. Ryan had each boy look into the magnifier. "Those marks are Arabic words and numbers. According to these books, what we have here is a dirham or silver coin made during the ninth and tenth centuries. Coins such as this one were traded in Europe, the Middle East, and even Asia."

Ben cocked his head to view the coin from a different angle. "That covers a lot of territory. I thought people back then stayed in castles or close to home."

"Most did," their mother said. "But some, such as the Vikings, traveled a lot by sea and along rivers. Vikings set up trading settlements in Greenland and along the Volga River, in what we now call Belarus. They even came to the east coast of North America. Lots of other places, too."

"Wow! They surely got around," David said.

"Because Vikings traveled a lot, they especially prized these coins for their value and beauty," their mother said. "The Vikings liked things that sparkled or were colorful. When this coin is polished, you'll see how pretty it is. The Vikings used and saved Arabic dirhams for bartering. Coins like dirhams helped them count how rich a person was. Sometimes Vikings would trade dirhams for gold chains and bracelets."

"Wow! I can't believe we found a coin hundreds of years old and from across the ocean," Ben said.

"Did you find anything else in the area?" Their mother had a quizzical look in her eye. The boys glanced at each other but kept their promise not to tell.

"We haven't had much of a chance to look. We found it when we were using Grandpa's metal detector," Ben said.

"Well, I'm going to make a couple of calls to some museums and researchers I know. You boys may become famous. This coin might have been part of a collection. Or, it may have found its way to Upper Michigan through fur trappers or Indians."

The boys left her to her phone calls and promised to be back before dark. They raced off to their "treasure place" on their trail bikes, this time with better tools and food in their backpacks. Ben and David hurried to the site, where they leaned their backpacks against a tree trunk. Besides the shovels and pulley, they had brought two trowels, a small ax, and a whisk broom. They crammed peanut butter and jelly sandwiches into their mouths and began digging.

Twenty minutes later they had the metal box almost uncovered. Ben convinced David to resist an urge to brush off the top until they got the box out of the hole. He wanted to enjoy the full effect of their discovery where they could see it in good light. They loosened dirt underneath two corners of the box. Ben tied a rope around each end. He threaded it through the pulley that David had tied to another rope, which was looped over a stout low-hanging branch above the hole. Their years of working on badges in Boy Scouts was paying off. Each boy pulled on a rope, and the box was hauled to the surface and pushed to firm ground.

David and Ben knelt next to the intriguing box. David reached for the broom and carefully dusted off its strangely carved metal top. As dirt and decayed matter were swept from the cracks, strange writing appeared. Around the edge of the box were long skinny lines forming different shapes and patterns. Ben was stunned. "David, you're not going to believe this! We've discovered real Viking treasure. You see those lines? Those aren't scratches. They're runes."

"What the heck are runes?" David asked.

"Mom showed me some in one of her books. Remember when I did that report on Leif Erikson last year? The Vikings had only a few letters in their alphabet—sixteen letters, in fact. They were lines that resembled sticks in various shapes. See here?" Ben traced a letter with his finger.

"Can you read any of it?" David asked.

"Not really. But I can read a name: OLAF. This looks like a Viking sea chest, and it must have belonged to a guy named Olaf."

"Wow! So maybe what mom said about Viking things being traded or collected is true?" David asked.

"Who knows, but let's open it," Ben said. The boys were so enthralled with the carvings that they almost forgot to check out the trunk's contents.

The leather hinges were rotted off. The metal lid was rusted, so the boys used their trowels like crowbars. Ben and David expected to find the chest empty. Finally after much grunting and straining, it was time to lift off the lid. They decided to do it together on the count of three. "One...two....three...lift!"

David and Ben gasped as they viewed the contents of the sea chest. It was filled with coins just like the one Ben had found earlier. There must have been hundreds of tarnished silver and glistening gold coins. This was beyond their wildest dreams. The boys thrust their hands through the cool, slick coins. Ben's hand hit something hard near the bottom. He was careful as he pulled the object out of the box.

"Oh, my gosh. I don't believe this. A real Viking dagger." Ben's fingertips carefully traced its handle. It was beautifully

carved with swirls and geometric designs. The end of it was shaped as a serpent's head, its eyes two small red stones that looked like rubies. It was an incredibly beautiful dagger.

Ben grasped the handle with his right hand as though he were its mighty owner. He slashed at an imaginary enemy and a swirl of dead leaves began to swarm around the two bewildered boys. The wind suddenly changed pitch as if a monster storm was blowing in from the lake. Its roar in the trees was deafening. A blinding flash of light knocked them down. Its heat was so intense that both boys thought they had been struck by lightning. But the commotion ended in a matter of seconds, followed by an eerie silence. Ben and David were scared out of their wits. What on earth was happening at their treasure place?

The stunned boys stood up. The sea chest was still there but the big oak tree was gone. David, his eyes big as saucers, looked behind them and whispered, "Ben, our bikes are gone, too."

Suddenly, just beyond a stand of pine trees came a deep bellowing shout. David and Ben grabbed their backpacks and scrambled for cover behind some nearby bushes. They watched as a large man appeared in the clearing. Well over six feet tall and muscular, he had a red beard and red woolly hair. He wore leather boots wrapped with laces and a long woolen shirt-like tunic tied with a leather belt. An ax hung from his waist, and a wool cape was wrapped around his shoulders He looked like the pictures they'd seen of Vikings.

The burly man shouted to someone in a foreign language. He took a leather pouch from his belt and dumped its contents into the open sea chest. More coins! It didn't seem to bother him that the chest was open.

What was going on? Who was this man? Why was he dressed like a Viking? The boys were about to sneak off when two more men emerged. Their hair and beards were a blondish color, but they spoke the same rhythmic language and were dressed in similar clothing.

Strange! The boys shivered as a chilly winter breeze blew through the forest. Summer had changed to early spring. There were tiny new buds on the trees and a haze of pink blossoms in the distance. A gust of wind clattered hundreds of cold grey branches like old bones.

Something caught the eye of the massive red-haired man: the blade of the dagger in Ben's hand was glistening in the sunlight. Without the protection of thick summer leaves, the boys had been spotted.

2

Trespassers

David and Ben were frozen with terror. Their trail bikes had mysteriously vanished, and they knew they could never make an escape on foot. The red-bearded Viking motioned to his companions and pointed toward the bushes where the boys were hiding. The three giants lumbered toward them. They squinted at the dagger in Ben's fist. David and Ben screamed and so startled the men that they also yelled. For a few seconds, everybody yelled at everybody else. Almost as quickly, they all stopped screaming and stared at each other.

The huge red-haired man said something to the others in Old Norse. The boys recognized the language because Grandma Peterson spoke Norwegian. Ben, who understood more Norwegian than David, whispered, "He said something about us being young boys and wonders what are we doing in their woods, and a lot of other stuff I didn't understand." The burly man was surprised to hear them speaking English. He knew several languages, one of which was Anglo-Saxon, an early version of English. (Although Ben and David picked up on Anglo-Saxon quite quickly, this book will use the modern English translation.)

"Where did you boys come from and what are you doing in our woods?" The Viking sounded menacing.

"*Your* woods?" Ben started to disagree.

"Hey," David elbowed Ben. "If it's their woods, it's *their* woods!"

The men assumed that Ben and David were there to steal the treasure. Several tense minutes passed before Ben was finally able to convince them that they were lost and that they had come upon this place accidentally. Ben learned he could make up a story rather quickly when a two-hundred-pound hairy guy was breathing down his neck.

The men stared and pointed at the boys. They had never seen jeans, T-shirts, and tennis shoes. They felt the fabric and wanted to know where they could get some. David and Ben whispered back and forth as they tried to figure out what kind of people had never seen jeans and T-shirts before. For now, they thought the three might be mountain men who had been living in the woods a little too long.

After the treasure was buried again, the three woodsmen insisted that the boys return to their camp with them. Neither Ben nor David had the guts to resist as they gawked at the hatchets, daggers, and thickly-muscled arms. The boys discovered that the red-haired man was named Olaf, the younger blond one was his assistant, Torgier, and the third fellow was their friend Vita. Together, the five of them tramped through the woods, occasionally stopping for food and rest. It was getting colder and the boys had no jackets. They wondered what happened to summer. And where were the sounds from the nearby highway?

When they got to the Vikings' camp, a crowd of surly men gathered around them. They jabbered in Old Norse and taunted the boys about their strange-looking clothing. They poked and prodded Ben and David and touched their clothes. Just a few of them spoke Anglo-Saxon.

How many mountain men were there, anyway? It appeared that they had brought their families out here to the woods of Michigan to create their own Norwegian village. How come Ben and David had never heard about this? The boys were sure they were both having the same nightmare. But they realized they were certainly not at home sleeping.

Ben and David were taken to Olaf's *grettir,* which is a large main house where the Viking *jarl,* or chief, lives with his family. There was plenty of room for many people. Unfortunately, Vikings also invited their chickens and cows inside during cold weather. Ben and David had to breathe through their mouths until they managed to adjust to animal odors in the house.

A servant greeted Olaf with a bowl of water. This Viking chief washed his face, ran fingers through his hair, and then blew his nose into the washing water. The servant proceeded to the next man. This ritual continued until every man had done the same thing, all using the same water. Ben and David were sick to their stomachs. They refused to wash up when the bowl was offered to them.

Olaf was a man who seemed to be in good humor most of the time, which was lucky for the boys. Olaf's wife, Gitta, showed them where they could sleep. She pointed to a pallet underneath a rafter of clucking chickens in a corner of the log room. The boys stared at each other in disgust.

Olaf asked them about their village, how they got lost, and lots of other things. David and Ben did their share of smooth talking, and Olaf seemed satisfied with their vague answers. They had lots of questions for him, but Olaf seemed confused and irritated when they asked. The boys tried to ask about the cabin's electricity, indoor plumbing, and television. Ben realized Olaf thought they were making fun of him. David turned to Ben and said, "You getting the idea we just might not be in Michigan anymore?"

"What is this Mitch-a-gin?" Olaf asked.

In the morning, Gitta awakened the boys. She gave them some warm clothes: leather leggings, fur and felt boots, a felt hat, a rough woven shirt, a woolen tunic, a belt, some leather and fur mittens, and a fur-lined cape. The clothes were a little big, but it felt good to be warm. Gitta insisted they put their old clothes in their backpacks. She was amazed at their backpacks' thin waterproof material. Her backpacks were made out of leather and were very heavy.

They ate a breakfast of black bread, dried herring, and some roasted pork. Then they were handed a big drinking horn of "mead." Their faces turned green as they stared at the sweet honey drink. Floating on top were maggots. Disgusting! Gitta laughed, took a wooden spoon and scooped them out. The brothers had no choice but to drink. They had already refused the washing bowl and to turn down more gestures of hospitality would be an insult and perhaps dangerous.

Soon after breakfast, Olaf rounded up the men and boys of the village. David and Ben stepped outside into much fainter sunlight than they were used to. At this time of year in the Land of the Midnight Sun, there were barely six hours of sunlight a day.

"Look!" David pointed to nearby snow-capped mountains.

"For sure, we're not in Michigan," Ben gasped. "Wow!"

Olaf approached Ben and David and said, "Today we are setting out for the port city of Bergen. It is a two-day walk from here. Then you will sail with us to Scotland. My son, Thor, and several other young people were captured by Hammel of

Dronninglund when he raided our village a few days ago. We must get our children back from him. If we don't, they might be sold to slave traders in Morocco. Many sheiks in North Africa desire slaves who are fair haired and blue eyed, so our villages are frequently attacked."

"Slaves? You've got...slaves?" Ben's jaw dropped.

"No. But people across the seas keep many slaves," Olaf answered.

"You mean 'slaves' as in 'serfs'? I've read about serfs," Ben said.

"No serfs here, either. Never in Norway! We don't have feudalism here." Olaf was irritated at David's puzzled look, but Olaf continued in a gruff voice. "In the Germanies, for example, serfs have many important rights spelled out in voluntary contracts. Slaves have no such rights."

"Which is why people have to be kidnapped to become slaves." David caught on quickly.

"Ya. After they are captured, the kidnappers sell them for the highest price they can get. Many slaves are children of slaves."

Ben pointed at David and himself. "We're not slaves now, are we?"

Olaf laughed. "Of course not. Strange? Yes. But slaves? No!" He put a hand on each boy's shoulder. "But I have a feeling that you boys can help us get our children back home. Will you?"

The boys glanced at each other and shrugged. It's not like there were options. "Sure," Ben said. "Don't know how, but we'll give it our best shot." Olaf clasped both boys around their shoulders in a hearty Viking hug. Ben heard his shoulders crack.

"Thank you. Thank you very much! We will discuss the details later. You will be on my ship. Your work will be hard. You will get food and supplies for the men and help make repairs. If our quest is successful, you and your brother can go back home."

This last comment confirmed their suspicion. This was not a joke or a dream. It was real....inescapably real. Bergen is in Norway, and Ben and David knew it is a major shipping port to all parts of the world. But centuries earlier, Bergen was a Viking outpost. Oh, these thoughts were mind boggling. Were they actually in medieval Norway?

Were these really Vikings? Somehow, they had been carried back in time to the tenth century. Ben tried to explain the events of the past few hours to his younger brother.

If Ben's explanations were accurate, how on earth would they ever get back home to Michigan? They were terrified.

3

On Board a Longship

The weary crew walked for two days. Thick pine woods finally started thinning. They hiked up a rocky ridge. Olaf pushed aside some tree branches to reveal a clearing. Below them lay the bustling port town of Bergen.

Rugged green hills sloped sharply into the water in most places around a large, irregularly-shaped harbor. The port itself was on the only reasonably level area at water's edge. The boys noticed it wasn't as chilly here.

As Ben and David stared at the town, they realized that somehow they had passed through a time warp. Instead of cars, there were horses, carts, and wooden sailing ships. There was no sign of electricity—no wires, no lights, no poles. Dirt paths led to the market square, the docks, and the merchant quarter. Everyone seemed to be speaking a different language: Old Norse, Finnish, German, and even Arabic. Despite all the old stuff, it looked like an exciting place.

Ben and David said little but saw a lot as the group entered Bergen. There were vendors' carts in one area with merchants selling or bartering handmade weapons, swords, shields, and gold and silver jewelry. Hand-carved statues of different gods were being sold for good luck charms. Some items they had seen in museums or photographs in their mother's archaeology books. There were carts of apples, breads, smoked fish, and cheeses.

David was shocked by the people's foul odor and filth. Some had missing teeth. The boys walked around in a daze trying not to overload on all the strange sights. Olaf clutched the backs of their cloaks and steered them toward the docks. He didn't dare let the boys out of his sight for fear slave traders would kidnap them, too.

David turned to Ben and said, "Hey, this really is Bergen. Look at the water. Anywhere else this far north, you can't sail the year around. And if we're really here, out there has to be where the North Sea and Gulf Stream meet the Norwegian Sea. Beyond that, it gets choked up with ice in the winter. Did you notice the trees when we were hiking down here?"

"Yeah," Ben said, "they were full of tiny green buds. This must be the end of winter, otherwise it would be dark most of the day. Since it's light only about six hours a day and dark the rest of the time, I bet it's around the end of April or the beginning of May."

With several Vikings watching them, they stopped near the shoreline and waited as Olaf paid for a new ship and for repairs done on another ship. Ben stooped down and dipped his fingers in the water. "It's cold!"

Olaf yelled for them to come. There were several small dinghies that would take his men out to the anchored ships. It was hard to tell which were Olaf's ships because there were so many masts in the harbor. They looked like a bunch of toothpicks bobbing up and down in the currents.

Ben and David timidly stepped toward the small boats waiting to be pushed out in the water. Olaf grabbed them by the collars and yelled at them to help push off from the dock and then hop in. The others laughed and shook their heads over the boys' inexperience. Ben and David clambered into the moving dinghy and moved out of the way so the oarsmen could row to the ship.

They reached Olaf's longships after weaving between the other longships and knorrs in the harbor. The longships were wide and shallow-draft, which helped keep them from tipping in rough waters. Over a hundred feet in length, longships could hold sixty warriors. Nobody could build ships like the Vikings. Merchants and seamen traveled to Scandinavian port cities from all over the world to buy Viking ships.

The men climbed onto the ships with their personal belongings on their shoulders. The sea chests had been hauled in earlier and placed in the deep cargo pit underneath the center deck planks. Ben and David were hoisted aboard by a muscular Viking.

Olaf gave them no time to catch their breath before he began ordering them around. "Boy! Over here. Get these barrels of water and mead fastened down!" Olaf shouted. When the supplies were battened down under a tarp in the pit, David and Ben retreated to a corner in the stem of the boat to rest. This was a tough, dirty, tiring business.

"I'm hungry, I have to go to the bathroom, and I'm already tired of being pushed and ordered around," David said. Just then, Olaf found them. He called them lazy dogs and ordered them to help get the sails out.

The younger men sat in rowing stations and used sea chests for seats—the same kind that Ben and David had been investigating when they were blasted back in time. Their shields were attached to the railing of the ship as protection from the cold sea spray that splattered in as they clipped through the water.

.s they exited the harbor, Ben and David looked back at the It was beautiful. It had tall pine trees and green hills shad- g the village and harbor. The docks were packed with thin ng masts and colorful sails of hundreds of ships from dif- countries. Merchants had arrived from warmer climates to trade with the eager Norwegians. The Vikings didn't have much farmland and were always short on fruits and vegetables. Since they didn't have spices, silk, silver, gold, or other exotic goods, they traded what they did have: honey, amber, mead, herring, codfish, and their ships.

Ben and David were already exhausted, and the trip had just begun. The ships turned southwest out of the harbor heading for the east coast of Scotland. The scenery was breathtaking. Ben and David had heard about the fjords. Now they had an up close view of them as the ships skirted the Scandinavian coastline, often passing between narrow mountainous islands and the coast as they headed toward Stavanger.

Steep rock cliffs covered in moss and new lush green plants were enshrouded by mist that fell from hidden springs and melting snows. The powerful surge of the sea seemed to move in slow motion. Their longships were like toy boats beneath imposing steep cliff walls. Seabirds cried and circled in the misty air overhead as they aimed for their nests that clung to rocky walls. The boys' attention was riveted to the spectacular scenery. "Sure beats Michigan, huh, Dave?" Ben motioned toward the view.

Hammel and his clan lived in Peterhead on the east coast of Scotland, directly across from the southern tip of Norway. It was a high rocky place where watchful eyes could spot any seaward approach. Peterhead was a lush green land smothered by fog in the mornings and evenings. Cliffs jutted out into the water and provided excellent guard posts over incoming ships. The humidity made everything grow wild and green in the summer. Wildflowers looked like they were painted onto the background.

When Ben and David were relieved of their duties, they were given a hunk of black bread and some dried fish. Even mead tasted good. They retreated to the stern of the ship and huddled together for warmth. The sea air was chilly, especially when the sun set. They were almost too tired to eat, but they knew they had to keep up their strength. When they had to go to the bathroom, they did what everyone else did: they hung onto a rope while hanging off the back of the ship, their legs dangling onto the deck. "I can't believe we are stuck in the middle ages." David's teeth chattered.

"I can't believe we have to go to the bathroom in the ocean," Ben complained. "I've never seen this in the movies."

"Or in history books," David said.

"At least we're not seasick like that guy over there." Ben pointed to one of the younger Vikings heaving his dinner overboard. The sight and sound of it made them nauseated, so they tucked the bread inside their capes and decided to get some sleep. Little did they know what adventures awaited them in Hammel's castle.

4
Hammel's Path

The pitching roll of the longship jolted Ben and David from their sleep. As they peered over the ship's side, the first light of dawn was creeping over the rolling hills of Scotland's east coast. Threads of misty clouds clung to the jagged high rocks. Hill-sides were dotted with woolly white sheep, and pastures were pieced together like a patchwork quilt.

Ben saw wisps of smoke rising from behind a high hill. "Look! That must be where the village is. See that smoke?" Both boys quickly ate the last of their bread from the night before.

"Boys!" Olaf yelled. "You have slept long enough. Do you cling to your mother's skirts at home, you good-for-nothing char-coal-chewers? Come and help take the sails in. Soon we will be landing and preparing to attack."

"Attack?" David was stunned. "Does that mean we have to go along or will they let us stay on the ship?"

"They'll probably make us go whether we want to or not. Olaf asked us to help get the kids out, remember?" Ben squeezed his brother's arm to reassure him.

Within minutes, all sails had been furled and tied down. The men were quiet. The only activity was that of oarsmen who rowed the longships toward shore. The water was choppy as they cut close to the cliffs to anchor. Vikings held their weapons as they prepared to lower the dinghies and scramble down short rope ladders. Olaf gave the signal. Silent men helped Ben and David into the dinghies. Like a colony of ants, they poured into the small crafts. Olaf noticed there was no alarm call. Fog and early morning darkness masked their entrance into the rocky harbor.

Even in a sheltered cove their ships would be spotted soon. The men had to be hidden in crevices and caves by daylight. Olaf spoke. "We will surround the village and attack from all sides as soon as Ben and David make it inside the camp and locate the children. Success requires everyone's cooperation."

"You want us to do *what*?" Ben and David asked in unison.

"You will sneak in as our enemies are waking. Find out where the children are located. Watch out for sheepherders. They wake early to get their flocks out to pasture. Remember: you cannot obtain your freedom without our children's freedom," Olaf said.

Ben and David were terrified. Olaf meant business. "We could be killed before we even make it inside the village. What if someone spots us?" As time-travelers, they could feel pain, hunger, and exhaustion. They knew they weren't protected from death.

Their climb up the cliff was grueling. Men had to be helped up the shifting rocks and slippery surfaces. They wasted many precious minutes of darkness struggling up the cliffs. Ben and David were to slip into the encampment before sunlight reached the valley. The eery dawn light and dewy fog played tricks on their eyes as they crept in a half crouch toward the camp.

Olaf was irritated. By the time his exhausted raiders approached edges of the settlement, it was already too light. When he peered through a long tube with a big piece of glass at the end, he became enraged. "The camp is deserted. No wonder there was no alarm call. All I see is old women and filthy animals. Where are the men and children?"

The men were silent as Olaf fumed about his missing son. Ben and David picked up their cue and walked in silence. There was only one thing to do now; they must attack Hammel's castle.

Painstakingly, they retraced their steps back down the cliffs. Since this was a rescue journey, they returned to the ships with nothing except their weapons. Olaf ordered everyone to pack food and water for two days. He was furious with Hammel. He wanted justice, and he wanted his son back.

The men were quiet as they prepared for the invasion of Hammel's castle. The two longships were left anchored in the cove. Several Vikings remained on board to protect the ships.

Back up the cliffs and through the sheep pastures, the men trekked cautiously. They reached the edge of a forest and spread out among the trees to watch for any sign of Hammel's men. The sheepherders were on the other side of the valley now, so the Vikings were not detected.

The tall narrow towers of Slains Castle could be seen above the treetops. The men were quiet as they peered at the distant stone and wood building. Olaf said, "I cannot tell how many guards there are so we must wait until we see some activity."

To safeguard against surprise attacks, each man had his own bird call to warn of approaching danger. After a couple of hours of watching castle walls and towers, Olaf gave two whistles. The men crept out of their hiding places. All reported seeing no more than twenty or thirty guards around the castle walls.

"Assuming there are more inside, we may have sixty guards to fight. That's about one for two of us. Even if there are more, we can handle it as long as we catch them off guard," Olaf said. "Eat in silence and rest until just before daybreak. It will be cold, so use your cloaks. No fires tonight. Vita and I will take the first watch, Sven and Torgier the second. No drinking. We cannot succeed with muddled brains." Everyone found a sheltered spot to rest for a few hours.

Ben and David studied the castle while the sun still shone on its outer palisade walls. They noticed the square *keep* with the tallest tower in its center. Hammel and his family lived there. It was defended by towers surrounding it. Ben noticed a couple of guards walking slowly along the parapet of a wall facing the woods. The castle was built near a rocky cliff overlooking a valley, so tunneling underneath was impossible. Ben and David gawked at high sheer walls with murder holes and narrow slits for bowmen. They wondered how Olaf planned to get inside.

David whispered, "This would be a great time for us to be zapped back to Mom and Dad and Grandpa. Maybe we have to die in this lifetime first or something. Are you scared about attacking the castle, Ben?"

"I've never been so scared in my life. What if we get an arm or leg chopped off, or worse? What if we have to fight a warrior? We don't know how to fight with swords. How did we get into this mess anyway?"

Ben and David slept fitfully while the Vikings kept watch. They were becoming more like Vikings. They could sleep so tuned into their environment that any noise triggered their reflexes to jump up with dagger in hand. Ben thought about how shocked their mother would be if she woke him for school and he jumped out of bed with a dagger in hand.

When the sky was a pale blue, Olaf gave each man his orders. Vita was scouting in the woods when he smelled smoke from a campfire and found a trail which led to the castle entrance. He ventured down a cart path and spotted three peasants camping. It was tax season so peasants traveled to the castle to pay their taxes in the form of grain, wool, hides, or other goods. These lowly folks had wagons containing grain and hay. Hammel's men would be in the woods guarding the trail from thieves and highway robbers. At dawn, the peasants would proceed to the castle.

Vita led the way on a winding road to the peasants' camp where their attack would take shape. The men covered their tracks by scattering leaves and brushing branches over footprints. Vita and Olaf were ready and eager, like horses before a race. They crept from tree to boulder to bush, scarcely making a sound.

It was still quite dark. Ben and David kept bumping into each other, which earned them a smack to the back of the head from Torgier. Suddenly an owl swooped down around their heads and screeched a warning. They were in its territory and it was upset. Their legs turned to jelly and their hearts pounded like bass drums.

Minutes later, Ben and David stopped in their tracks when those leading the way froze in place. All was deathly still; they smelled smoke from the peasants' campfire. Ben and David felt strong hands on their shoulders urging them to crouch down on their knees and wait with the other men while Vita, Torgier, and Olaf left on their mission.

A few minutes later a robin's whistle echoed faintly through the trees. Sven answered with his blackbird call, and they were on their way again. They crept in silence. They watched for Hammel's men. Stars in the sky behind them were fading but those in front were still twinkling.

Ben and David, aware of the vital part they were to play, grew more anxious with each step. One little mistake could mean the end of their lives.

As they reached the campsite, Vikings gathered around Olaf, Vita, and the carts of hay and grain sacks. The peasants had been knocked unconscious, gagged, and tied to a tree. Their mules were hitched to the wagons. David crawled up on the front seat of one wagon next to Vita. Ben sat with Torgier and Hans sat next to Olaf. The men removed grain sacks and hay bales from the carts to hollow out the middle of each heap. Quickly they climbed in and filled the hollow. The remaining men piled the hay bales and grain sacks around them to hide them from view.

Olaf, Vita, and Torgier acted like peasants from nearby villages. Ben and David were their sons. Hopefully, they could smuggle half the Vikings through the castle's front gate. As soon as the attack was underway, Ben, David, and Torgier were to run to the gatehouse and lift the portcullis to let the other Vikings in.

The Vikings said a quick prayer to Thor, the god of war, and were on their way. Ben and David remained silent. All weapons were hidden under their seats within easy reach if needed. The three carts rattled forward.

Torgier had his cloak over his head. He hunched over in the seat to appear poor and sickly. Ben and David coughed for special effect. Guards stopped them at the barbican, a small gate before a main gate. Guards, swords in hand, looked them over.

"What village are you from?" the suspicious chief porter asked. He decided who gained entry and who was denied entry. Without missing a beat, Torgier answered, "Just down the road. From Ellon. My neighbors and I are bringing our tax grain for Hammel, the great warrior, to feed him and his courageous men. He protects us from our enemies. We have brought our best grain and fodder. It makes the tastiest bread and strongest beer."

Torgier gave the chief porter a wink and a smile. The official seemed satisfied, but his hairy assistant decided to look under the cart. Olaf had decided it would be too dangerous for any men to hide underneath the wooden axles. A wise decision. The guard looked puzzled and walked to the back of each cart. As a distraction, Torgier started to talk with the chief porter about his best beer recipe. The other guard inspected and probed until he was satisfied. Another sentry waved to the gatehouse.

Gatehouse guards responded to their comrade's signal by turning the winch that lowered the drawbridge and raised the main gate. Torgier chirruped the mules while the drawbridge creaked into place. The three carts had moved only a short distance when, suddenly, the hairy guard yelled at them. "Halt!"

5

Hide-and-Seek

Torgier debated whether to make a run for it or to stop. They had no place to run. How fast could they go with a load of grain, hay, and seventeen warriors in a beat-up wagon being pulled by two dumb mules? He decided to halt and act puzzled. The hairy guard caught up with them and said, "Look here, peasant. You had better take care of this." Torgier gave the reins to Ben and stepped down. He dragged himself to the back of the cart, limping and feigning illness every step of the way. He was sure the guards could hear his heart pounding. What had the guards discovered?

As Torgier turned to face the wagon, he exhaled a sigh of relief. The guard had stopped them to warn them of a split bag of grain. When Torgier's cart had jerked on its way, the grain began to pour out from a hole in one of the bags and left a trail along the path. Torgier pretended he was terribly grateful that the guard had saved some of his precious grain. He told him he would report the favor to Hammel himself. With a tuft of grass, Torgier plugged the hole in the grain sack and hoisted himself aboard the cart once again. The old mules trudged forward over the drawbridge. Whew! They had passed their first test.

Ben and David fought the urge to hold their noses as they drew closer to the moat. A giant can of air freshener would have been welcome. The water was a muddy putrid brown color, not deep blue with exotic fish swimming as depicted in movies. Then they saw the source of the smell.

On the castle walls were chutes that came down from inside and emptied stuff into the moat. The moat was little more than an open sewer filled with waste from toilets, kitchens, and the castle's garbage. But what an effective defense. Who would want to wade through that muck to get inside the castle?

Inside the portcullis, the main gate, were two more guards to inspect the entourage. They were forced to wait inside a holding room while the guards asked questions and checked with people inside the castle as to whether or not they were expected. Behind them the heavy wood and iron gate closed with a thud. They had made it inside. Now what?

The boys' gaze moved toward the ropes and pulleys from the series of gates to where the rigging disappeared into holes in the ceiling. They stared upward and were stunned. Looming right over their heads were the murder holes, just as they had seen in books about castles. They could see and hear guards in the guardhouse overhead. Ben wondered what was piled next to the holes over their heads. Boiling oil? Balls with spikes? A load of sharpened stones? Whatever it was, the boys didn't want to find out. One thing they knew for sure: the murder holes were appropriately named. Ben and David were terrified that they would be discovered and murdered on the spot.

What was taking so long? Finally, a guard returned with confirmation of their appointment, and they were led inside the castle wall. This was it! Imposing steep towers loomed over their heads. The carts jerked to the center of the bailey or courtyard. A servant woman stood at a well. A horse was being led to the stables by a squire.

They heard the clinking sound of the castle blacksmith forging some new weapon or tool. No one paid much attention to their group until someone shouted at them. It was the brewer. He motioned for them to take their loads of grain over to the woodpile that was stacked outside his door.

The castle seemed to be almost deserted. But it was a sizeable fortress. Ben and David knew that at the sound of an alarm, warriors would swarm into the bailey ready to fight. They wondered if Olaf had guessed correctly how many there were.

David stared up at the *keep*. He tried to catch a glimpse of Hammel, his wife, or anyone standing on a balcony or peering through a narrow window slit.

All castle treasures were kept in the bailiff's chamber. David pictured heaps of gold coins and chests of jewels. The bailiff's chamber was one of the most difficult rooms to reach. It could be entered only through the master's chambers. Usually there was a secret wall or hidden passage that concealed the way to the master's chambers. The trick was to find that secret entry while you were busy defending yourself against castle guards.

David was terrified about the prospect of sword fighting, but he was thrilled at the thought of finding treasures. He had only read about such adventures, and now he was actually going to have a part in one. The reality hit him like a punch to the stomach. He nudged Ben and looked up at the top of the keep. Ben knew exactly what David was thinking. This would be a turning point in their lives.

Torgier led the way toward the brewer, who was impatiently waiting for their contents.

"Here, here! There she goes! Easy now, mind the woodpile," he shouted to the Vikings. The brewer counted the bags of grain, sampled some from the ripped bag, and gave his first sign of approval—a smile. It was clear by the look on his face that the grain was of superior quality. He beckoned Torgier, Olaf, and

Vita inside the brewery where he gave each a tax receipt with Hammel's stamp on it.

Once out of view, Torgier took matters into his own hands. With his ax handle, he quickly bashed the poor brewer on the head and dragged him behind some bags of grain. Outside, Ben, David, Vita, and Olaf struggled with bags of grain as they removed them from the carts. Torgier returned to help. In a matter of minutes the Vikings were off the carts and inside the brewery.

With weapons ready, the first order of business was to take control of the guardhouse where the drawbridge could be lowered and gates opened to let the remaining Vikings inside. Olaf surveyed the area while the others stretched their aching muscles.

Outside the castle, two road guards were tied up and removed from the guardhouse's view. Sven and Olek had taken the guards' cloaks and weapons and put them on. Sven was short and Olek was tall, so from a hundred yards away, they looked much like the guards. Under cover of bushes and boulders outside the main gate, dozens of Vikings waited for a signal.

Olaf, Torgier, and Vita moved cautiously into the courtyard in three areas: behind the well, a woodpile, and a stack of barrels. Ben and David thought it was a lot like playing hide-and-seek up to this point. No one had died yet, there were no bloody fights, and everyone still had all their arms and legs. So far, so good.

Olaf and Torgier clutched their weapons and crept across the courtyard from the brewery to the stairs under the guardhouse. No alarm sounded. They made it without being detected.

After waiting a few minutes, five others quietly took their positions behind Olaf and Torgier. As stealthy as cats, they tiptoed up the log stairs to a room over the main gate. All seven Vikings were at the guardhouse door gripping a log by its carved handles. Ben and David watched breathlessly from the room where the brewer remained unconscious.

BOOM! BOOM! BOOM! The battering ram splintered the guardhouse door. The guards scrambled for their weapons, stunned that they were being attacked from inside the castle. Hammel's guards were shouting, jumping up, and running into each other. It was sheer chaos.

Ben and David quickly took up their assigned positions to watch and warn the Vikings if other guards were coming from the courtyard. Swords collided with shields which deflected potentially fatal blows. With shields and helmets in place, it was difficult to tell who was who.

The fighting was mostly slow and clumsy. This was nothing like the dashing sword fights Ben and David had seen in movies. They were disappointed by the sluggish action. Unfortunately, though, blood would be shed and real lives were at stake.

Ben and David caught flashes of red streaking by the dark wood wall. Castle guards jumped from a guardhouse window ledge to the courtyard since the stairs were blocked by warriors fighting. Guards in towers shot arrows at the Vikings. Ben and David had a perfect view of the fighting, but they scrambled for shelter under some stairs to avoid dangerous projectiles.

Once everyone was out of the guardhouse, it was the boys' turn. After loud clashing of swords and smacking of fists, Olaf and his men had subdued Hammel's guards on the stairs. The guards lay bent and broken like toy soldiers. Olaf and Torgier joined other comrades who were fighting for their lives. Ben and David had their orders. They crept carefully over the wounded guards nudging them with their feet to make sure they were unconscious. They had never seen so many bodies.

"Quickly! You two have work to do," Olaf shouted. Ben and David regained their concentration and ran upstairs to the drawbridge machinery. They heaved and tugged, grunted and groaned until they finally managed to lower the drawbridge and raise the front gate. This was the signal the other Vikings had been waiting for. They charged! They sounded like a thundering herd of buffalo as they tramped over the moat, their heavy weapons flailing and their shouts filling the air.

Vikings charged into the castle courtyard in the nick of time. The stable guards had alerted other castle warriors. Another heavy wood and iron gate protected Hammel and his family inside the *keep*. Olaf's blood surged with anger. He shouted the order to charge ahead, and the real fight began.

Vikings thundered up the stairs, two at a time, and quickly brought down three guards. They had an advantage. Not only were they fueled by anger and revenge, but the element of surprise was on their side. Olaf's plan was to attack full force before Hammel's guards had time to get their bearings.

The Vikings used all their strength and wits to battle Hammel's men. So far, less than thirty minutes had passed since their entry to the castle grounds. While one-on-one fighting was slow and deliberate, the battle was fast and deadly.

Ben and David left the guardhouse and moved to the well. Since the guards' helmet visors blocked their field of vision, Ben and David managed to creep by them, trip them with boards, and knock them out with their clubs. Surprise was the name of this deadly game.

Two of Olaf's men had leg injuries. The wounded men were dragged up the stable stairs and into the other guardhouse since Hammel's men had left to join the fight below.

"This could be checkmate time. They've left the most vulnerable part of the castle unprotected," Ben said.

"I bet they thought they'd get us with arrows and assumed there were guards still inside the gatehouse. Or maybe we just surprised them into fighting without thinking. Boy, we were lucky!" David pulled Ben behind a stack of barrels.

Sven and Torgier smashed open a door and went straight for the winch. Hand over hand they turned the winch's wooden spokes. Finally, the *keep's* gate shuddered and creaked open. It looked like the mouth of a great giant yawning after a long sleep. Once all the Vikings were inside the *keep,* Sven and Torgier rushed to lower the gate. They could hear angry shouts and heavy footsteps of guards closing in on them. Olaf and the men shoved their way inside the *keep's* guardhouse and through the heavy oak door. The foxes were in the chicken coop!

"Hurry. Hurry up. They are almost here," Torgier shouted. They hadn't lowered the gate all the way, but only a foot of space remained between the floor and the bottom of the gate. Suddenly, two guards charged forward shouting for others to follow. One tried desperately to hold onto the gate and lift it, but it was too heavy. The other guard shot arrows through the bars.

The gate finally shut with a resounding thud. Sven and Torgier worked feverishly to dismantle the ropes and chains while they dodged arrows. On the outside was a secret panel which could allow the gate to be lifted in case of emergency. The ropes had to be cut to prevent Hammel's guards from using the emergency entrance. Using their shields to block oncoming arrows, the two Vikings hacked at the ropes with their swords.

Outside, guards grunted and cursed as they tried to crank up the gate by hand. Torgier was desperate as he worked on the last rope. Then with a creak and a snap, the gate came crashing down. They had done it. The gate could be opened now only by using a battering ram to smash through it.

Two arrows were stuck in Sven's shield. One was hanging loosely from the back of his mail vest. Sven and Torgier turned for the *keep's* main door just as an arrow went clean through the fleshy underside of Sven's forearm. He shouted in pain. Together they pushed open the thick heavy door and barricaded it on the inside. The shouts of Hammel's men became muffled cries as the door shut behind them. Arrows hit the wood with twangs and thuds. The Vikings could hear the clash of swords echoing in the cold stone hallways.

"Give me your arm, Sven," Torgier said. Sven dreaded what was coming, but he knew his arm would be permanently damaged if he didn't do what Torgier said. Sven put the blade of his sword in his mouth and prepared to bite down.

Torgier took Sven's arm in one hand, braced himself against the wall, and placed his fingers around the feathered end of the arrow. He quickly snapped it off. Sven grunted through clenched teeth. In one quick motion, Torgier seized the other end with the arrow head and pulled. Sven's eyes grew large and sweat poured from his face as the broken arrow slid from his forearm. He bit down on the blade and tried to muffle an agonizing scream. The worst was over. Torgier wrapped Sven's arm in a strip of cloth from his tunic. Sven took deep breaths. They must move on.

Sven now held his sword with his left hand and put his shield over his wounded right arm. They rushed down the passage and around a corner. Noise was coming from the Great Hall.

Long tables were set up end to end and made a U-shape in the middle of a large room. Brightly colored banners with Hammel's coat of arms on them hung from poles fastened to the wall. A brilliant red lion and a great hunting dog, signs of courage and loyalty to the laird, were featured in the middle. Those symbols had to be earned and were awarded by the laird.

A huge chandelier the size of a small swimming pool hung from ceiling timbers. It held dozens of dripping tallow candles. Ben and David were overwhelmed by the room's size and decorative colors on the walls. Rich tapestries hung on the stone walls to help keep the chill and dampness out of the huge hall. Ben and David crouched in the shadows behind a pillar that supported a balcony. They watched the Vikings fight their enemy.

Torgier and Sven arrived just in time to see several guards go down with a clamor. Guards in full armor were at a disadvantage against the quicker Vikings. Their cumbersome armor was heavy and hindered movement. When a guard was knocked down, he became an easy target.

Torgier looked up and saw several lightly-armored guards scurry from the balcony to hallways. "They are trying to hem us in. Move out before they close the doors," he yelled.

Ben noticed one of the tapestries featured a fascinating hunting scene. He wondered how anyone could weave such a giant carpet. Then he noticed something, and asked David if he saw anything unusual about a second tapestry. David stared at it.

"Yeah! It's moving at the bottom. You think somebody's hiding behind it?"

"Nope! Better than that." Ben feared nobody wanted to hear a boy's ideas, but he knew he had to try. "Hey," he shouted to Olaf. "Bet that's the way to Hammel's private rooms."

6

Labyrinth

With several dozen Vikings looking on, Ben led Olaf over to the tapestry. Ben was shaking and sweating. He wished he had checked it out first before saying anything. But he knew castles. He had seen diagrams, studied their designs, and read a lot about castles. He just had to be right!

With David's help, he managed to push away a heavy corner of the tapestry. A light breeze blew through cracks between the rocks causing the tapestry to sway slightly. Ben felt a breeze as his fingers followed the outline of a small doorway. He pushed several stones until he found one that opened a secret door.

Olaf and the others were stunned when they saw a hidden passage. They wondered if Ben was inspired by Norse gods. Olaf smiled for the first time in days and showed his appreciation by slapping Ben on the back…hard!

The door opened slowly with a grating noise, like fingernails scratching on a chalkboard. The cramped passageway was dusty and dark. The men had to enter single file and stoop down to avoid hitting their heads on the low ceiling.

Someone grabbed a couple of torches from wall sconces in the Great Hall. They shut the door behind them. Their only light was from the flickering torches.

When they came to a staircase, Ben noticed it ascended clockwise. This gave a defender descending those stairs the advantage. A right-handed soldier had more room to swing his sword going down the stairs, because a center pillar blocked the enemy's sword as he tried to move upward.

Torgier held a torch as he took the lead. A second torch was held by a man in the middle of the line so light was more evenly distributed. They crept up the staircase in silence. Every cough, every whisper, every sound resonated against the stone walls.

The line of men extending down the stairs resembled a snake that coiled around and around a tree trunk. After climbing for several minutes, Sven arrived at an arched wooden door. "How odd. Why would a secret passage have a door that so obviously led right to Hammel's quarters?"

Olaf leaned his ear against the door to see if he could hear anything. Silence. His men passed word of the door down the line. They must be prepared to defend themselves. Ben and David were terrified. There wasn't much light and no room to fight. And they were too far up the line to retreat. They were stuck!

Sven and Olaf quietly lifted a heavy wooden arm of the door. They peeked through the keyhole into blackness. Sven took the torch from Torgier and stepped aside. Torgier lifted his sword, and Olaf followed him with his shield and sword in position. Every Viking was prepared to fight as soon as Torgier opened the door. What was in store for them?

It was pitch black inside. Torgier took the torch from Sven and moved it around in an attempt to see where he was standing. A gasp escaped his lips as he stepped back. His eyes were wide. "I have heard of such things but I have never seen it before.

There are stairs and walkways everywhere, yet they go nowhere. See for yourselves, but you must stay against the wall. Be very careful. You go. I will stay here and guard us from the rear."

But Olaf snatched the torch and insisted that Torgier go with him. No Viking was allowed to show fear, especially none of Olaf's men. Torgier wrenched his arm free and refused to lead. So, Olaf went on ahead visibly disgusted with his companion. As soon as Olaf crossed the threshold, he gasped and quickly stepped back inside the doorway. Somewhat embarrassed, he ordered two men to accompany him. Now the others were curious as they elbowed their way through the small doorway.

Olaf held the torch in front of him so the others could see. They saw a labyrinth of staircases and walkways, just as Torgier had reported. Many of the walkways were at least partly suspended from chains and ropes, like bridges. They went every which way to many dead ends. Down below the labyrinth was a deep cavern. Olaf dropped a rock, and they waited to hear it hit bottom. There was no sound from the depths.

Each walkway was very narrow and the one leading from the doorway had no railing. Above and below were several dozen cascading walkways. Olaf held the torch over his head and stared into the depths.

"I have heard of these mazes. People can get lost in them and starve to death. It is another defense weapon in some castles. One has to know exactly which walkways to take because most of them are dead-ends or lead to a mortal trap. There must be dozens of them in this tower."

Torch light bounced off the wooden undersides of the nearest walkways and disappeared as the tower rose into obscure blackness. The terrified men wondered where to begin the search.

Olaf chose Ben and David to go with him to investigate the walkways. After all, the boys had been the ones to discover the entry in the first place. Besides, to Olaf it seemed like the gods were with these young people.

David removed felt-tip markers from his backpack. He told Olaf to leave a trail of markings so they could find their way back to the passageway. Olaf marveled at the dark paint that came from a piece of hard felt. He drew on his hands and arms with it. It was magic. It would make a good trail marker. Ben and David knew they had seen the last of that pen. They wanted to laugh as they looked at Olaf with black streaks all over his arms. But nobody laughed at Olaf—at least not if they wanted to survive. The men asked Olaf to paint lines on them, too, but he snarled that this was not the time for a tattoo party.

Clutching the remaining torch, Olaf gave the signal. Olaf, Ben, and David began their search for the entrance to Hammel's chambers. The other men stayed glued against the walls.

"The outside of the tower didn't look this big to me. How could they hide a labyrinth inside it along with all those other rooms?" Ben asked.

"Castles are full of mystery and intrigue, boy. Looks can be deceiving. The towers are tall and narrow in the front, but they're often very deep. Towers play tricks on your eyes like the crafty spirits of the underworld," Olaf replied.

They had walked a few yards and approached a cutoff, so David made an X with his marker. They turned to look back at Torgier and the others across the chasm just as enemy guards appeared three levels down from them.

"Torgier, you and the men must come with us. We have the marking stick. We'll lose them and be able to return to the passage faster than they will. Come quickly!" Olaf shouted.

Some panicked and almost lost their balance, but one at a time they filed onto the suspension bridge over the chasm.

"Divide into two groups. Boy, give them some of your marking sticks. Make your marks close to foot level so Hammel's men will not notice," Olaf ordered. David handed Olaf two more markers from his pack, and they quickly moved on. Arrows flew their way, but in the dim light there were few targets.

After an hour, Olaf, Ben, and David had moved down only two levels and up three. They finally arrived at the top level of the labyrinth. They had to be near the entrance now, but they still couldn't find it.

Hammel's men were close enough to hurl rocks. Their arrows flew past the Vikings. Olaf was tempted to cut down some suspended walkways but decided that was too risky. They might need them to get out.

Arrows and stones thumped against shields and walls. Some bridges looked like porcupines with arrows imbedded in the wood. Shouts and curses grew louder as the battle heated up.

Exhausted, Olaf and the boys collapsed against a wall. Ben glanced over to the wide open mouth of the labyrinth and wondered how deep the black hole was. He looked again at the network of bridges and walkways stringing through each other like Christmas lights. There had to be something there, a clue to the labyrinth.

Suddenly, church bells chimed announcing mid-morning mass. At that exact moment, sun rays reflected through a cross that had been cut out of stone high up on the wall. It provided the only light inside the labyrinth besides the torches. But the light shining through the cross provided a lifesaving clue. The sun's beams in the shape of a cross corresponded directly to two walkways that intersected and formed a similar cross. They were angled so that they caught the sun's light. But the sun would only stay in that spot for a few minutes. The long end of the cross pointed directly to a door that they had somehow missed. Ben pulled Olaf down to his eye level.

When this solution to the labyrinth was revealed, Olaf ordered Torgier to go towards the sunlight and to follow those two paths. Olaf, Ben, and David got up to run to the cross, but the lighted walkways immediately disappeared. Once they stood, other walkways from the labyrinth obstructed their view and the cross light vanished. They discovered that the cross was visible only from a kneeling position, so they crouched every few steps to see if they were headed in the right direction.

Unfortunately, Hammel's guards had figured out what the Vikings were up to. The guards raced Olaf's men in an attempt to reach the secret door first. Every few steps the guards stopped to shoot their arrows and then continued the race. Two Vikings were hit in the legs and shoulders, but their wounds were not life-threatening. As the sunlight shifted higher away from the cross, Olaf was frantic to reach the doorway.

"Hurry! We must hurry. The light of the cross is disappearing," he shouted. They raced along the walkways and crisscrossed paths with each other in their quest to reach the right level. "There!" He pointed to the door. Olaf jumped over a railing and down to the next ramp for fear of losing sight of the door. The others ran down the ramp, terrified they might jump the railing and fall into the dark abyss.

Olaf, Ben, and David neared a tiny door. From a distance, they couldn't judge its size because everything inside the labyrinth was designed to fool you, even your eyes. As they got to the door, they were startled to see it was only three feet high. Wedged into a dim cave-like entrance, one could walk right by without seeing it. The heavy wooden door was reinforced with rusted iron bars.

Olaf tugged at the black curved iron bar that was the door's handle. Nothing happened. He grabbed the handle, let out a loud grunt and yanked with all his might. Finally, the door's hinges creaked and the door opened.

7

Bailiff's Chamber

Everyone strained to see inside. Hammel's men were closing in on them. The Vikings had held them off with sling shots, swords, and arrows. With the dwarf-sized door halfway open, Olaf shoved his men through it one by one. The torch they had carried from the Great Hall was about to burn out, so they quickly lit torches lining this new passageway's walls.

With the last man in, Olaf raced up the circular stairs looking for Hammel's private quarters. There it was—- a door! Soon, the sound of that door being bashed in echoed through the stone stairwell. Olaf, at the front of the line, was eager to be the first into Hammel's chambers. The door was kicked in and there, behind a large wooden table was Hammel.

Hammel of Dronninglund stood in front of a large open balcony with his hands behind his back. With an indifferent look on his face, he stared at Olaf and his men. He seemed to have been waiting for them. He was short and stocky; his blond hair was so light it looked almost white. His eyes were a transparent blue that seemed like a liquid. He was wearing a heavy red velvet cape over his leather tunic. A knife and sword were at his side.

He knew that if he used either weapon he would be slashed to ribbons by Olaf's men in a matter of seconds.

Olaf stared at him with eyes glowing like hot coals. His rage erupted like a volcano. He pointed the tip of his sword at Hammel's throat and hissed through clenched teeth, "What have you done with the children of my village?"

The Vikings barricaded the heavy door to Hammel's headquarters. Enraged guards in the corridor pounded on the door as they bellowed obscenities. They tried to open it with a battering ram. The Vikings did not have much time. Olaf held his sword across Hammel's throat and dragged him closer to the door. Terrified, Ben and David cowered in the shadows.

"Remove yourselves from this tower at once or your master will be killed!" Olaf shouted at the top of his lungs. Silence. Then he heard mumbling.

"How do we know you have not already killed him?" a guard shouted.

Olaf looked at Hammel and said, "Tell them now to do what I say, unless you have nothing to live for."

There was a short pause until Hammel issued an order. "Listen to this pirate and do as he says. Leave the tower or he will run me through with his sword. Leave NOW!" More whispering. Then the sound of footsteps retreating down the stairs. Olaf released Hammel and ordered him to sit in a chair while Torgier tied him to it. As Olaf questioned Hammel about the children's fate, Ben and David began their own investigation.

"If we could find the bailiff's chamber with all its treasures, Olaf would have a great bargaining tool with Hammel," David said. "Those guards aren't going to go along with Olaf's wishes for long. He can't kill Hammel or he'll never find his son. I bet the guards are already coming up with a new plan."

The boys searched the walls. David remembered from his book on castles that the bailiff's room was usually next to the master's or family's chambers. Ben looked under the wall tapestries, but this time he struck out.

"That would be too easy," David said. They felt around the fireplace and ran their hands across the wall. Nothing. They were discouraged. Ben had an idea.

"We didn't check the fireplace."

"Yes, we did. We touched every inch of that wall and found nothing," David replied.

"No, I mean inside the fireplace. Come on," Ben whispered.

Olaf looked up and shouted to Ben, "Hurry up, boy! Find the entrance to the treasury."

Ben's entire body was inside the fireplace. "I've got something here. It's an iron handle." Ben pulled with all his might. Whoosh! The flue opened. Black soot and ashes covered his head. Tired and tense, David started to laugh hysterically.

Olaf was furious. "What are you two doing? Playing games? You'd better find the way in or you'll soon meet the pointed end of a guard's sword."

Ben shook the ashes out of his hair and shirt while David settled down and joined his brother. They reached along the inside wall of the fireplace and found another iron handle. Both pulled on the count of three. They moved aside to avoid more soot.

David and Ben jumped inside the fireplace just as it began to turn around. It was big enough for two or three people to stand in. They felt like they were on a spooky ride at an amusement park. The fireplace floor creaked and scraped as it turned like a revolving door. Within seconds, Ben and David found themselves in the treasury staring at the bailiff.

A tall skinny man was hunched over from his years of counting money and valuables. There were huge volumes on his desk in which he recorded the castle's treasures and inventory. A melted-down candle flickered dimly in its holder. He was dressed in a long cape similar to Hammel's with a long flowing robe underneath. He was old and wiry and had wisps of white hair that stuck out in every direction making him look like a warlock. Even his bloodshot eyes appeared wrinkled.

Ben and David were staring at his dirty bare feet when the man abruptly withdrew a knife hidden beneath his cape. The boys screamed in unison and reached for the fireplace handle. They both grabbed the wrong one and the flue opened and dumped more soot on them. Panic stricken, they wiped soot out of their eyes and groped around for the right handle.

The bailiff looked like a madman with his long hair flying in all directions as he lunged for the boys with his knife. Fortunately, his old bones weren't quick enough.

"Hurry!" Ben shouted as David pulled on the handle. Ben seized a poker to fend off their attacker. With the slow motion of a bad dream, the fireplace turned just as the bailiff reached them. He had to retreat or his hand would get crushed in the disappearing fireplace. The boys breathed a sigh of relief when they found themselves on the other side in Hammel's chambers.

"Quick! We found the treasury. The bailiff came after us with a knife. He's probably hiding all the money right now!" Ben and David shouted in turn.

Olaf and the others scrambled to the fireplace dragging Hammel with them. Ben and David were shoved out of the way while Olaf, Hammel, and Torgier crammed into the fireplace. Ben showed them which handle to pull. With a jerk, they were off to the other side. The fireplace returned empty. Three more climbed in until all the Vikings were on the other side peering at mounds of glittering treasures.

Ben and David watched in shock as greedy Vikings filled their pockets, pouches, and backpacks with gold and silver coins, stolen chalices, crosses, necklaces, rings, and an assortment of odds and ends from the castle treasury.

The brothers resisted temptation to join in. They had learned by the time they were three that they better not steal even a penny. Olaf was trying to control the mob, but they were trained to raid and pillage, just as Hammel's men were.

Olaf demanded that Hammel reveal the whereabouts of the children. He threatened to steal everything in the treasury and burn the castle down if Hammel did not confess. But Olaf knew that Hammel was buying time. The old bailiff had escaped and no doubt had alerted guards to the enemies' location.

Olaf had to act quickly. He heard the guards' shouts as they climbed the stairs. He tied Hammel to the bailiff's chair and took out his short knife. He placed it against Hammel's throat and hissed, "My men have already stolen from your treasury. We have defeated your warriors. We will get out alive and take your treasures. You have two choices: I can kill you now or you can tell me where the children are and continue your life with most of your treasures intact. Which will it be Hammel? Life or death?" Olaf pressed the knife against Hammel's throat even harder causing some blood to drip down Hammel's neck. Vikings stuffed their bags and pockets with precious booty. Some stood in front of another door ready to do battle.

The scene was like a nightmare for Ben and David. Before this time-warp experience, they had seen nothing worse than fights in the school yard. The boys covered their eyes and waited for Hammel's scream. But it never happened. Hammel wisely decided to reveal what he had done with the children. He said in a shaky voice, "They have been sold to Yusef, a goat trader in Egypt. He is a wealthy sheik in the Cairo marketplace. The children probably will be sold to slavers in Africa and the East."

Olaf glared at him as he returned his knife to its holder on his belt. He ordered his men to put back whatever they would not need for expenses on what now would be a longer journey than expected.

Before the Vikings left the bailiff's chamber, Olaf gagged Hammel's mouth and blindfolded him with a torn part of his shirt. Olaf grabbed Hammel by the hair and said, "If you do not speak the truth of this incident, my men and I will return to put an end to you and your family. It may be months or even years, but I will track you down like a wolf tracks its next meal. Do you understand?" Olaf released his grasp when Hammel nodded. Olaf cut the rope that held Hammel to the chair, tied his hands behind him and shoved Hammel in front of him.

"Open the door!" Olaf shouted. If the guards were going to shoot, the arrows would hit their master first. Olaf had turned Hammel into an insurance policy. He would use Hammel to usher them safely down the stairs and outside the castle walls.

As the door opened, bows and arrows were raised. "Put down your weapons. Our laird is their captive," the leader shouted.

"Let us pass without bloodshed, and we will release your laird when we exit the postern gate." Olaf had taken Ben's suggestion. The postern gate was in a wall at the rear of the castle and usually not heavily guarded. The guards retreated downstairs.

Torgier and Vita made sure the path was clear. Hammel remained in Olaf's tight grip, and Olaf kept the knife resting across Hammel's throat. Eventually they reached the bottom of the *keep.*

Outside in the bailey, Olaf shouted to Hammel's guards. "If any of you shoots a single arrow or hurls one stone, your laird will be put to death. Who wishes to be responsible for his death?"

Olaf and Hammel were surrounded by the other Vikings who flanked them in a circle, protecting them like bodyguards. With weapons ready and senses keen, Olaf and his men finally passed through the postern gate. Hammel's guards stood atop the castle walls watching his every step, but no weapon was fired.

Vikings melted into the woods around the castle without further incident. Hammel was released unharmed, as promised, and the Vikings vanished before the guards could hunt them down.

8

Bound for Egypt

By dawn, the exhausted Vikings retrieved their ships from their camouflage of seaweed and fog. Tempers were short. Once they were out at sea, they examined their plunder. As they headed toward the English Channel, laughter was heard amidst the clinking of valuables and the counting of coins.

Olaf and the boys stood at the bow. "Can we make it before slavers take the children who-knows-where?" Ben asked.

"We have to." Olaf's jaw set. "We just have to! But it's going to be close. We cannot waste any time."

As the two longships rounded the rocky coast of Galicia, they kept within sight of the shoreline. The Moors, who were of Arab and Berber descent from northwest Africa, had been in control of most of the Spanish peninsula since 711 A.D. They had conquered all but the northwest corner, which was known then as Galicia. Although there were no fierce Moors here, Olaf knew that after the ships passed Galicia, they would encounter them somehow.

The Galicians were a hearty stock of fishermen and goatherds who did not take kindly to foreigners stealing their land. Olaf told Ben and David about the skirmishes that beat back the Moors each time they tried to conquer Galicia.

"The Moors don't want anything to do with people that live off the land because they think only animals do that. They simply want what they haven't got, and it makes them angry to keep losing it." Olaf sneered and then laughed. But he admired the Galicians because they fought for what was theirs, just as he was fighting to get back the children who were kidnapped from his village. He waved to some Galicians in fishing boats, and one of them sounded a greeting from a horn.

It was then that Ben noticed something unusual. "Look at the surface of the sea," he said to David. "Do you notice anything different about this water and the land?"

"Not really." David did not understand Ben's point.

"Well, open your eyes! Not one bit of litter or pollution. There isn't even a film of oil on top of the water like there is on our lakes and oceans. Look how blue and clean everything is."

"Yeah, you're right. Wow! Just think. We're getting to see what the earth looked like before plastic bags and other nondegradable stuff were invented." David was impressed. They cherished the sight of unspoiled land and water.

Curious about which direction they were sailing, the boys took compasses out of their backpacks. They stood by the rail on the starboard side and studied the little dials as the needles stopped spinning. Olaf was intrigued when he saw the boys hunched over something.

"What is going on here? Olaf asked. Startled, David almost dropped his compass.

"We just want to know where north is and which direction we are sailing," Ben answered.

Olaf grabbed the small glass and metal instrument and shook it. The dial spun around and Olaf stared at it with wide eyes. "What is this?"

"Oh great! He's never going to believe this," David said.

"It's a compass. The needle always points toward north to the magnetic North Pole, so it pulls the needle towards it. If you line up the "N" for north with the needle, then we know which direction we're heading," Ben explained as best as he could.

"What is mag-net-ic?" Olaf asked. "How does the needle know where to point?" Olaf was skeptical. He compared it with his compass, which was called a *solarstein.* It was a crystal-like rock that he held up to the sun. When it became opaque or cloudy, he could plot their direction using the sun's location during the day and the stars at night. Olaf discovered that the boys' compasses were far less troublesome than his *solarstein*. He yelled at Torgier and the others. "Come quickly! Look at what the gods have sent me. This will make sailing much easier for us."

"Oh, no," David whispered, "he thinks it's his now."

"Excuse me, Olaf, but the gods gave that to *me.* They say we should take care of it if we are to help you get your son and the others back safely. They say we will need it, and that is why they have given it to us. You don't want to anger Thor, the god of the sky and thunder, do you?" Ben was catching on to Viking ways.

After discussing it with Torgier, Olaf returned the compass without a word. Olaf continued to stare at the boys in either amazement or fear. They couldn't tell which.

Olaf shouted to his shipmates that the ships must tack farther out to sea as they headed toward the southern tip of Spain, which was Moor territory. Ben and David looked at each other and wondered how terrible the Moors were since Olaf was avoiding them. They believed Olaf could scare the pants off anyone just by glaring at them.

A sudden gust of wind caught the sails and caused Ben and David to lurch against each other and tumble to the floor. No one made a move to help them. Olaf shouted for them to get up and act like men. Ben saw the look on David's face—terror. Ben felt sorry for his younger brother. He hated to see him so frightened. He caught David by the arm and pulled him to his feet.

Just then, Olaf took Ben by the back of the neck and shoved him toward the rigs and ropes. "Help with the sails, you lazy dogs! Have you no sense between the two of you?"

Ben and David moved toward the stern and tried to look busy. They wondered if Olaf had forgotten all they had done to help defeat Hammel's men in the castle. David's fighting spirit came back. "Who does he think he is? Christopher Columbus?"

Ben laughed. "I doubt it. Columbus won't be born for at least four hundred years." That reminder shocked them. Wide-eyed, they gave each other a now-familiar look of disbelief.

It took another day to reach Al-Andalus at the southern tip of Spain. Ben and David were munching on stale black bread and eating the last of their ration of salt-cured fish when Ben realized where they were. They were passing Gilbraltar, a narrow little trading port at the tip of the Spanish peninsula. It seemed to be crawling with dark-skinned Moors who wore turbans and flowing white robes with colorful sashes. The boys strained their eyes as they tried to pick out details on shore. Sunlight reflected from long scabbards and knives many Moors had hanging from their waists. They saw no children. Only a few women were outdoors. They were covered in black cloth from head to toe. Olaf was busy shouting orders to his men.

The Vikings raised a special banner. A symbol on it indicated that they were passing by for trading, not to raid or attack. They were relatively safe here since trading ships from all over Europe and Asia often traveled these waters. Even so, Ben noticed several men on horseback keeping up with them on shore, never taking their eyes off the Viking ships.

Olaf looked through his spyglass. With scorn in his voice he said, "Those dumb Moors. They think they can catch my ship on horseback? I never saw a horse that could swim." He turned to the boys. "Don't worry about those Moors. They have no skill on the water. But on land, it's another matter. They are like one with their horses."

The other Vikings nodded in agreement. A Moor on horseback was a powerful fighting machine, especially in a saddle with stirrups. It was the stirrups that combined horse and rider to make the use of weapons far more deadly and effective. Moors were excellent warriors and could kill with one swift blow while galloping on their Arabian stallions. Olaf admitted Vikings were no match for them on land. But the Moors were no match for the Vikings at sea. So the Viking longships sailed by Gilbraltar and into the Mediterranean Sea with little caution.

Ben had been scurrying around like a ship rat looking for extra food when he overheard Olaf telling Torgier they were headed for El Mansura and then on to El Qahira. They planned to stop in Tripoli, Libya to get more supplies and food before heading for El Mansura.

Ben and David knew that El Qahira is Cairo in today's world. It became El Qahira when Muslims from Tunisia captured it in 969. Since the boys knew that the Vikings had become Christianized by 1100, they figured they were stuck in time not long after 969.

David huddled in a corner at the stern fighting a bout of seasickness. He looked up at his big brother and muttered weakly, "When are we going to get off this ship? It seems like we've been on it forever."

"I know, but hang in there. I just heard that we're going to be stopping for supplies in Tripoli, which is only a couple of days away. And then, we're going to pass through El Mansura at the mouth of the Nile River and on down to Cairo close to where the pyramids are. Maybe we'll get to see them." Ben was trying to distract David and lift his spirits.

"We're never going to get off this ship, and we'll never rescue those other kids. I just want to go home," David moaned.

"Did you do what I told you to do?" Ben asked.

"No, I haven't been able to move."

Ben helped David move to the starboard side of the ship. There he could look at the passing coastline. "Now, block one ear and just stare at the land. I guarantee that within a few minutes your seasickness will be gone." Ben left David and went to work so Olaf would not come looking for them.

When Ben returned about a half hour later, David was like a whole new person. "You were right. I feel a lot better. Where did you hear about that?" David asked.

"I read about it in one of Dad's medical journals. Motion sickness has to do with the balance of fluid in your inner ear. You trick your brain into thinking that your balance is level by letting it get the message from only one ear, so you block the other ear. When you look at the horizon or something stationary in the distance, your brain gets the message that you are actually stable. So you start to feel better. Motion sickness really is all in your head," Ben explained.

Within a few days, the longships docked in Tripoli. What a sight. Strange singing filled the air throughout the whole city. To Ben, it sounded like Tarzan trying to sing an opera. When they got closer to shore, Olaf explained that the sound was the Muslim call to prayer. Muslims pray five times a day. They have a chanter (or muezzin) who stands on a minaret tower and leads prayers through a horn that makes his voice louder. All citizens stop what they are doing and kneel facing toward Mecca.

Olaf explained that Mecca is their main holy capitol, sort of like Jerusalem is for Christians and Jews. Nothing keeps most Muslims from their prayers. "They even stop fighting a war to kneel down and pray," Olaf said. He laughed with scorn. Clearly, he neither understood nor appreciated their religion.

"How would you like to have to pray like that five times a day, every day?" David asked his brother.

"No thanks. That, plus having to kneel wherever you happen to be when that guy starts bellowing through his horn. Can't you just see us kneeling on the baseball diamond during a game?"

Before the Vikings began to get into their dinghies, Olaf instructed them to leave on board all ale and mead and to keep their pagan religious items well hidden. The Muslims had a death penalty for anyone caught drinking in public or intoxicated. They also didn't take kindly to other religions, but they would be tolerant as long as people were there to do business.

Ben and David were scared when they heard all this talk about killing and how Muslims didn't like non-Muslims. As their dinghies approached shore, it became clear why the Vikings would honor Muslim customs while they were in Tripoli. Hundreds of knife-toting Muslim men were visible.

The boys were amazed by the different customs and manners. In Tripoli's main *souq* or marketplace, they were surrounded by men shouting, their fists raised in the air. All were trying to get the best price or the best quality for some item to trade.

It was like a three-ring circus. The atmosphere was thick with excitement. Ben and David were mesmerized by the loud voices, hand signals, and heated arguments that were all a part of how business was done here. But no one ever got into a fight. When the yelling was over, each man took his winnings. They would embrace, then go their separate ways.

"It's like the whole thing is nothing but a show," David said.

"Yeah! Did you see that? Those two guys over there looked like they were about to punch each other over that fish, and they ended up hugging. Weird, but interesting, huh?" Suddenly Ben looked sad. "I wonder what our friends are doing this summer. I bet they're not having as much excitement as we are. But I'm so worried about Mom and Dad and Grandpa."

Olaf tapped Ben and David on the shoulder. "Young people are often kidnapped off the streets of Tripoli and sold into slavery, especially if they appear to be lost or unescorted by adults. So stay close by us." What a switch, Ben thought. A week or so ago, we thought the Vikings would kill us. Now we are relying on them to protect us.

As they moved through narrow dusty streets of the *souq*, the boys noticed that the dark, bearded men in turbans glared at them with obvious hatred in their eyes. Ben and David thought the men were wearing dresses. But in the heat of north Africa, long shirts, called *galabia,* and loose-fitting pants were cool and comfortable. The collarless shirts and pants were white or light colored. The only color was in the turbans they wore. Ben and David were intrigued by the carved and jeweled knives some Muslim men wore at their sides. These were usually worn by high-ranking men, so only a few possessed one. Others carried less ornate scabbards that were hung at the waist with a belt or sash.

Men sat and drank thick Turkish coffee at outdoor cafes in the main part of the *souq*. But no women were to be seen.

They rounded a corner. Ben and David heard chattering and loud whooping as they came to the women's market. Like hundreds of talking dolls wearing veils and black *chadors,* the women gossiped and bargained for goods. They moved expertly through the crowds with their children in tow and baskets upon their heads. Only their eyes showed through a slit in the veils.

"Those outfits must be awfully hot to wear," David said.

"Since they all wear the same things, I doubt they have much choice in the matter," Ben responded.

"Why do they wear those black head veils and long robes with long sleeves? Black absorbs more heat than light colors."

"I don't know. It doesn't seem to make much sense when it's this hot." Ben wiped sweat from his face.

The women moved quickly and quietly away from the Viking men, diverting their eyes and lowering their gaze. The presence of Ben and David was not threatening to the women, but the Vikings made them nervous.

Olaf and his men bartered for things they needed to continue their journey: breads, fish, fruits, and jugs of fresh water. A few Vikings traded some shields and swords they had worked on during long winter months to sell for Arabian dirhams. Olaf let the boys examine a coin just like the one they had brought to their mother. It had the same markings, but it was shiny and new.

"These are the same coins Mom was telling us about." Ben pointed to several more in the Viking's hand.

"She was right. The one we found is Arabian," David said.

The episode caused both boys to feel a surge of homesickness. Had their family sent out search parties? Did they find their bikes? Ben felt an ache as he thought of his mother weeping over their disappearance. Was time passing in Michigan like it was for them here? If so, they had been missing for about two weeks. The thought frightened them.

Ben and David ran to catch up to Olaf and Torgier as the Vikings returned to their longships. They overheard Torgier tell Olaf of his talk with a one-armed beggar in the *souq*. The man's son had helped haul provisions to some ships less than ten days ago. He'd seen a dozen light-haired children on one ship, several wearing clothes like Torgier's.

The Vikings were gaining on the slave traders. But, could they catch them in time?

The Viking longships lurched and rolled in rough seas. Ben and David sat against some sea chests and leaned on each other for support and comfort. The winds whipped around them and sea foam splashed over the sides. To protect themselves, the brothers made a small tent from one of their capes and used the other one as a blanket. Their knapsacks became pillows.

Rain pounded the deck. David and Ben thought they were going to be sick. They tried to get to the center of the ship and down into the pit. Everything was slippery and there was nothing to hang onto. It was like being in an earthquake. Every time they tried to grab onto something, the object moved out of reach, and they went flying in another direction.

Ben yelled to David to crawl on all fours. David was right behind him when Ben was finally able to grab the edge of the pit where the tarp was tied. He swung his feet around and planted them inside on one of the steps. He turned and grasped David's hand just as the ship pitched again. David was tossed toward the port side. Ben held onto his brother's hand and pulled as hard as he could to haul David down inside the pit with him. It worked.

Both boys trembled. Rain poured into the pit, which was designed to be a storage bin for protecting supplies and valuables, not a shelter for men. But it was the safest spot to be while the men were on deck lashing down supplies and taking in the sails.

The sudden storm had blown them off course toward a Mediterranean island. At dawn, everything looked so beautiful and clean that it was hard to believe there had been a storm a few hours earlier. Fortunately, nothing or nobody had been washed overboard in the squall. They were lucky this time.

The Mediterranean Sea was a deep blue-green. Ben and David peered over the edge and watched hundreds of fish swim by in flashes of colors. They were awed by the water's clarity and rich turquoise color. A group of dolphins followed the ships in search of discarded scraps. It was fun to watch them jump and play in the water like children on a playground.

The boys were fascinated by the distant islands, some so small that nobody lived on them. There were islands with short stout olive trees crowning their surface and white-washed houses dotting the landscape. Some of the islands had cliffs. Ben and David wondered how people got up there in the first place, especially to build a house. Then they saw an old man with a donkey slowly climbing up a steep rocky path. What would it be like to have to get to school by donkey every day?

Fishing boats threaded among the islands searching for sea bass, shrimp, and other edible fish. The boys yearned to go swimming, especially since they hadn't bathed for weeks. Since that was not an option, they leaned over the rail to catch the spray from the waves that lapped at the ship's sides. Cool water felt good on their dirty arms and faces. Their clothes dried in the morning sun. The ship shifted as it tacked starboard. They were back on course for Cairo. Slowly, the quaint little islands disappeared from view. The boys' attention turned to what lay ahead for them in El Qahira.

Olaf ordered Ben and David to help carry sea chests out of the pit. Easier said than done. The heavy chests contained the men's belongings including items they made during winter for barter in foreign markets. Vikings hoisted chests on their shoulders and marched up the ladder steps. With a lot of heaving and grunting, Ben and David finally managed to drag one trunk onto the deck. By now, the men were accustomed to the two weaklings and usually ignored them. Some still made fun of them and yelled at both brothers when they were in the way. After several weeks on the ship, the boys had learned when to speak up and when to make themselves scarce. When the trunks and crates of food were on deck, Ben and David were ordered into the pit to bilge out the remaining water, which was filled with bits of crud and dead bugs. David stood on the ladder while Ben waded in the filthy water with a bilge scoop. The routine was to fill the scoop, hand it to David, who gave it to a Viking. It was passed from man to man until the water was tossed over the ship's railing. After a half hour of scooping, rags were used to finish mopping up the mess. The pit finally dried out. Chests and crates of food were returned to the pit.

Ben and David retreated to the stern. They found a spot between two large crates where several wet capes had been hung to dry. They crawled underneath the capes and imagined it was a cozy dry tent in their Michigan woods, a great place to sleep. Both boys had been fond of camping out, but now they longed for a warm bed with clean sheets. They promised themselves never to ask their parents to go camping again.

Olaf had given them some extra bread, dried herring, and mead. He said they looked too skinny and needed to put on some weight. The boys finished eating and fell asleep against each other in their temporary tent.

9

Land of the Pharaohs

Wisps of cool sea breezes whipped Ben's hair around his face. David pulled his cape closer to his body. It was almost summer, but it was still cool on the open Mediterranean Sea. The longships had reached the mouth of the Nile River

The Nile Delta, where tributaries of the world's longest river fan out and spill into the Mediterranean Sea, was an exciting place to be. It is the only major river in the world that flows north, moving from higher ground in the south "up" to its Mediterranean outlet. Nile waters churn a yellowish brown and look like chocolate milk being dumped into the deep blue sea. The water carried with it desert sands picked up over thousands of miles, rains from the African plains, and runoff from many different countries. Even back then, the Nile supported life for tens of thousands of people, as well as animals.

As their ships approached the harbor of El Mansura, the travelers could see torchlights reflected in the water. They had plotted their course from the north star, which never "moves." Their colorful sails were fully open. Oars were placed into their positions around the rail. Each oar had a ring around the handle end to prevent it from slipping into the water through its hole on the railing. Ships needed both sails and oars to move upstream against the strong Nile current.

The longships anchored offshore at El Mansura in a cove where the current was much weaker. Anchors were weighed and sails taken in for the night. Two guards stayed awake on each ship to warn of danger. As always, Vikings slept with weapons ready at a moment's notice. Even Ben and David had gotten into the habit of sleeping with one hand on their daggers. It was the Viking way and, for the time being, they were Vikings.

The brothers were anxious about Cairo and the next day's mission. Soon, with a gentle breeze and easy rocking motion of the ship, everybody was sleeping peacefully except the guards, who fought only sleep that night.

As the sun peeked over the eastern shore, the men were up and ready to go. Olaf peered at El Mansura through his long viewing horn. He decided it wasn't worth making port there since there was very little activity other than fishing. They headed upstream through the mirky waters toward Cairo, just a few miles south.

The shallow-draft longships were perfect for navigating waters like the Nile. It was easy to maneuver around obstacles such as logs, crocodiles, sandbars, a dead cow, and flat reed barges of river dwellers—a real smorgasbord of debris.

Some people were eager to move out of the way when they saw the impressive longships. Others screamed and shook fists at them for invading their part of the river. The wakes created by the ships' oarsmen almost capsized several river barges drifting in calmer waters. Olaf and the others laughed and ignored the plights of the these unfortunate people, but Ben and David were embarrassed and did their best to avoid the scene.

By mid-morning, the ships approached Cairo's harbor. Even in the tenth century, Cairo was larger than any other town on their journey. Many ships were anchored in the harbor. Merchants were here to do business and trade goods for exotic things from the east and Asia. There was an aroma of cinnamon, curry, and tobacco.

Olaf peered through his long viewing horn and the boys wondered what good that could possibly do. The thick crude glass was scratched and cloudy. They smirked every time he used it. "We will anchor here and row in on the dinghies," Olaf told his crew. Torgier signaled Olaf's order to the other ship.

Cairo's harbor was crowded with ships of all types: from flat river barges loaded with food and poultry to bulky Chinese junks carrying loads of silk. "Have you ever seen so many colors and shapes?" Ben shouted to his wide-eyed brother.

"Look at those sails over there. They must be from Japan or China, judging by the strange characters written on them. The sails look like they're made of paper," David said. "Look at those bright blue ones with yellow stripes."

"This harbor is jammed with boats. How are we ever going to get to shore?" Ben asked.

"I have a feeling people will get out of the way when they see Vikings coming!" David laughed. At that moment, Olaf shoved both boys toward the dinghies.

The trip reminded Ben and David of snakes weaving around the steep sides of these big ships. They worried that their dinghy might be crushed between two ships as they rocked in the current. They were grateful these experienced Vikings knew how to maneuver dinghies safely though the shadowy wall of ships.

As they rounded the stern of a Greek trading vessel, a bustling harbor burst into view. Its colorful striped tents and cloud-white plaster buildings reflected the bright morning sunlight.

Ben and David scrambled out of the dinghy and hurried to land—firm dry land at last. Suddenly, they both fell flat on their faces. Olaf and Torgier laughed until they cried. Ben and David were experiencing what Vikings called "sea legs." They had become so used to the ship's constant pitching that it was now hard for them to stand on land. Their sense of balance would take several days to return to normal. In the meantime, the boys stayed close to Olaf and each other for support.

When Olaf and his band walked through the city, laughter stopped, conversations ceased, and cold hard stares came their way. To protect their mission, it was obvious that they needed to be on their best behavior and stay out of trouble.

Ben and David tried to ignore the stares. They were eager to take in the sights and sounds of Cairo. They made a game of identifying foods by smell if not by sight. Many items were new to them such as spices in their raw forms: cinnamon bark, nutmeg seeds, and saffron branches. In their kitchen at home, these spices were in little bottles bought at the store. Not here. One man was selling long knotty beige things that turned out to be ginger root.

A foul smell filled their nostrils as the Vikings turned a corner. David held his nose. Just then Ben's foot hit a squishy slippery pile in the street. It was camel dung. They looked up just in time to see a camel driver approaching. He shouted angrily at his camels. Ben and David quickly jumped aside as the camels trotted through the thick crowds knocking down anyone in their way. There were dozens of the one-humped camels jostling and pushing their way along the dusty market road. They caused a big racket as drivers tried to control the herd with long sticks and lead them toward a penned-in area.

Bedouins from the Sahara Desert brought camels here to trade with other nomads or herders who needed to replace aged or

sick camels. It was exciting to watch the procession and hear noises of camels and drivers heading toward the *souq*. At the end of the camel line, a cloud of dust settled over market tents.

Ben and David came to a shaded cove between two market stands. A small wiry man was sitting on a straw pallet with a recorder-like instrument in his hand. He was dressed in a ragged long white *thobe* and gray pants and wore a turban on his head. He appeared to be blind in his left eye, which was covered with a milky-white film. His bare feet were wrinkled and dirty and his toenails were yellow and curled over the ends of his toes. As he blew into the instrument, he moved his head at the basket set in front of him. The boys listened to him play for a couple of minutes and, suddenly, out of the basket rose the head of a king cobra.

Ben and David stood transfixed, wide eyes staring at the cobra. "I'm afraid to move or look away. What if it comes after us?" Ben said. The cobra's head seemed to mimic the old musician's, and they swerved together in time with the music.

"Cool! How does he do that so the cobra doesn't strike at him?" David whispered.

Olaf joined them and said, "I don't know what kind of magic they have here, but it is powerful. Don't ignore or laugh at it."

"I get the idea that Vikings think everything is magic," David whispered to Ben.

As they rounded another corner in the *souq,* Ben and David saw several belly dancers entertaining a group of curious spectators. Twinkling coins were tossed on the ground in appreciation of their skillful dancing. The brothers were amazed at how the dancers moved their bellies and hips without moving any other part of their body. The strange whining music and their beautiful costumes were appealing. The boys had seen something like it at a circus, but this was much more impressive.

Vikings stopped to watch the belly dancers, but they became so rowdy that several Egyptian men shouted at them. Olaf signaled for his men to move on before there was trouble.

Once again, Ben and David were impressed by how the important purpose of their journey unified the Vikings and headed off trouble. Olaf spoke the motto they'd heard several others use: "Remember our children!" Every Viking shared the same purpose: they were there so that they could rescue the children from slave traders. Nothing could be allowed to get in the way of accomplishing that purpose.

Behind the dancers were several toothless old men sitting cross-legged on the ground. Their *thobes* were dirty and their eyes were yellow with age, but they seemed content to smoke their water pipes and gossip about old times.

A few feet away was a man selling *laban,* a rich buttermilk drink made from goat's milk. Olaf thought it would be a good idea to buy some and inquire about Yusef, the goat dealer. Olaf bought enough *laban* for several men and passed Ben and David a cup of their own. They really didn't want to drink it because the same cups and dishes were used over and over without being washed. People did not know about germs back then.

Rather than offend Olaf, the boys drank up. Much to their surprise, they actually liked the drink. It was much thicker than milk and tasted a little like yogurt with a hint of sweetness.

Olaf's men passed around some fruit they had bought. Melons, bananas, and grapes were delicious with the thick creamy *laban.*

It had been so long since they had eaten anything but dried fish and hard bread that their taste buds almost exploded with joy. They savored each bite. They would not have a treat like this for a long time. The boys also knew fresh fruits were necessary to prevent scurvy, a fact unknown in the tenth century.

As they munched on the food, Olaf wandered around the area where goat cheese and milk were being sold. He began asking questions. Soon he had his answer. Yusef was known to be a very rich goat dealer, and he would be bringing in his goats behind the camel pen today. The man who told him the news was not pleased to be around a Viking, so he offered no other information.

Olaf took the boys aside and described his plan. He would treat Ben and David like slaves he had captured in a raid and came here to sell. Once they were sold to Yusef, the boys would try to get near Thor and the other children to devise a plan for escape. Understandably, the boys were fearful of this dangerous plan.

There was little time to dwell on their fears because they were suddenly grabbed around the neck by *souq* police. The Vikings were surrounded and captured. The crowd yelled at them in a foreign language. Ben and David were terrified and wished they could be zapped back home to their own time. Were they going to be executed?

Ben, David, and the other Vikings were crammed into a dark stone room. Several had tried to fight their way out but were restrained with ropes. They must have been knocked unconscious because their heads hurt and the last thing they remembered was being arrested in the *souq*.

One of the Arab policemen spoke a little Anglo-Saxon. He yelled at Olaf, "You and your men have stolen much food from the *souq*. You also arrived with weapons, which means that your intentions are hostile. You will be executed at dawn."

How would they ever get out of this mess? Escape was their only chance, since persuading the police or getting a lawyer were out of the question. Ben pulled David closer to talk over a plan. It had to work.

10

Desert Dwellers

As policemen came to herd them into the criminals' square, Vikings surrounded Ben and David. They silently pulled back to reveal two small shapes cloaked in blankets. It was dark except for torches held by the policemen. Vikings' dark shapes bounced off the walls creating an eery sight. Just as policemen tried to force the Vikings to leave the cell, two grotesque misshapen faces suddenly lit up from the two cloaked figures.

Ben and David chanted in unison in their deepest voices, "You are to let these men go. Whoever seeks to do harm to them will live the life of a flea on a camel's back."

The policemen gasped as they heard the two creatures utter their curse. Ben and David had created the scary effect by holding their flashlights below their chins to make their faces look spooky. Neither Arabs nor Vikings had any idea what had really happened. They assumed it was magic or some kind of spell. Policemen scrambled over one another as they rushed to the exit.

While Ben and David were putting on their ghostly performance for the police, others loosened the ropes that bound some Vikings. They dashed out of their cell down the hall to the guards' room. There, all their weapons stood stacked against the wall.

The men took but a few seconds to retrieve their swords and daggers. Then Olaf led them down a dark, musky corridor.

Their hearts pounded as they ran quickly but silently. They saw a shaft of light shining down from what looked like a tunnel opening. Olaf and Torgier stood underneath it listening for street noises. They heard nothing.

Olaf and Torgier hoisted Svenka on their shoulders to peer through an iron grate. He was eye level with a curving stony trail. The iron grate was easily moved aside, so it was probably some type of drain rather than a security device. Olaf cautiously pulled himself through the square opening and studied the area. One by one, the Vikings squeezed through the opening and took cover below the sloping trail. They were outside a big fortress overlooking the market.

They hid behind scrubby olive trees and boulders waiting for dusk. Just then, a dozen men in robes and turbans rounded the corner and scattered past them on the rocky trail that led down to the town.

Under cover of twilight, the Vikings made their way to the market streets. They walked alongside a herd of camels while the police searched for them on the other side of the street. The Vikings hid their weapons under their capes and wound linen shirts around their heads like turbans. As they tagged along with the camels, the disguise seemed to work.

After a lengthy trek, they slipped away from the camel herd and did not look back. Olaf hoped that everyone had followed his lead. Small groups of Vikings joined Olaf over the next hour until everyone was accounted for. They had come a safe distance from the *souq* and were at Pyramids Road. Olaf knew that Yusef would be coming this way with his new herd of goats. They waited behind a sand dune and drank from their water skins. Soon it would be night and they would get some relief from the daytime heat. In desert areas, nighttime temperatures dropped into the fifties, so their capes would come in handy.

They saw no sign of Yusef, so Olaf assumed they had missed him while they were detained in jail. He was angry about the setback, but more determined than ever to press on.

Ben and David found a spot behind a dune and lay down to rest. Ben couldn't get comfortable, so he got up to see what was making him squirm. He yelled. He was lying on a sidewinder. Ben despised snakes and kicked it as far as he could. David teased him. "That was only a harmless desert snake, Ben. I've never seen you jump so far so fast."

"I don't care what kind it was. I hate snakes! They're gross and disgusting," Ben complained. He settled down and within minutes was asleep next to his brother. But the desert's silence disrupted Ben's sleep. He lay awake for a while, fascinated by millions of brilliant stars. He wondered if their parents and grandparents were sitting on the beach looking at the northern lights over Lake Michigan. Or, were they out looking for them? They could all be looking at the same moon and stars and yet be thousands of miles apart. His heart ached as he thought of his parents. They must be in pain over their sons' disappearance.

Ben dozed off again until the sky began to turn a faded blue and the stars seemed to shut off for the day. Olaf roused everybody. They passed around some black bread, fruits from the market, and water that had not been confiscated during their short jail time.

They'd have to find shelter soon or they'd die in the sun-baked desert without protection. Within thirty minutes, the temperature began to climb. They were about to learn when to travel in the desert. By noon, they had to stop and set up their capes as makeshift tents against the burning sun. As twilight cooled things down, they traveled by the light of stars and moon. The Sahara is much kinder to foot travelers at night.

For many days, the Vikings walked upriver along the Nile as they searched for Yusef and the children. They bartered for food, water, and goats' milk from herders' caravans. None had actually seen Yusef, but some had heard he was heading south toward Upper Egypt.

Olaf encouraged the men to speed up their long, grueling search for the missing children. Viking chieftains' usual method for motivating better effort by their men was a promise of rewards upon their return to Norway. Such promises of riches coupled with Olaf's temper had worked before. But this time their united sense of being on such an important mission made such promises and threats unnecessary.

A couple days earlier, Ben thought he had seen the tops of some pyramids. They must be past Giza and Memphis by now. So exhausted, thirsty, and hungry from their grueling hike, Ben and David didn't care if they ever saw pyramids. Vikings were unaccustomed to the intense heat, so tempers flared easily. They prayed for a quick and happy ending to their mission.

While trudging upriver along the Nile's west bank, they found a pair of river barges. After much haggling, the owner traded them for several gold necklaces and some dirhams. The barges were long flat rafts made of reeds lashed together with leather, bits of wood, and vines. They had no sides and flexed with the waves. Getting on board was tricky. There were pockets of crocodiles concealed in reeds and muck along the river banks. The crocs waited silently for an unsuspecting victim.

Ben and David stepped onto one flexing barge. Nearby some water buffalo were cooling themselves in the water. Just as Ben reached out a hand for David, they heard an awful scream, thundering hooves, and splashing water. Ben and David watched in horror as a baby water buffalo's back leg was caught in crocodile's jaws. The desperate calf pawed at the muddy ground relentlessly with its front hooves trying to escape up the riverbank, but the crocodile was stronger and craftier. They watched as the crocodile savagely rolled its victim in the water until it drowned. Then in a frenzy, the crocs devoured the young water buffalo, head and all.

Vikings jumped onto the barges as fast as they could. The rafts were so overloaded that a corner of each dipped dangerously into the water. Some had to get off. Those men would have to walk the rest of the way to Thebes. Olaf told them to join the barge-traveling Vikings at the market in Thebes in two days.

Still shaken by the water buffalo's death, the men picked up barge poles and pushed the rafts upstream toward the Valley of Kings, where Yusef supposedly was camped. Fearful eyes scanned the riverbank for crocodiles. These Vikings had never seen such beasts. Those on the edge of the barges kept their weapons ready. Nobody dangled feet over the rafts' edges to cool off.

Within a couple days, the barges stopped on the Nile's west bank. The Vikings were anxious to get off the barges. The weary group had a surge of energy when they saw the market. They had run out of food and water. Ben and David hurried to keep up behind a trail of fluttering capes and lengthy strides.

Like Cairo, Thebes was a thriving city and had been the center of the Egyptian kingdom for many centuries. The Valley of Kings is west of Thebes. This is where many important pharaohs and priests were buried in underground tombs. Egyptians had learned centuries earlier that pyramid tombs were inviting targets for thieves. They quit building the immense structures when they discovered that many of their country's treasures had been stolen from the pyramids.

The Thebes *souq* was smaller than the one in Cairo. People from the countryside and farmlands seemed to be even tempered and more tolerant of foreigners than Cairo citizens. So their job of loading up on food and supplies was easier. They found breads, fish, meat, and fruit. David and Ben bought some goats' milk after discovering that it tasted like a malted milk shake. They drank while eating fruit, sweet dates, and figs. The boys filled leather pouches with fresh water from the market well. The Vikings bought as much food as they could carry for the journey west. Olaf had never been this far inland in Africa, so he had no idea how vast the Sahara Desert was or the dangers that lay ahead.

While waiting for the rest of their crew to finish shopping, Olaf and Torgier went to see the goatherds. They were determined to stay calm so the herders' suspicions would not be aroused by their questions about Yusef.

Ben and David stayed behind with the other Vikings while Torgier and Olaf pretended to be in the market for slave children to serve on their ships. Finally, they found a goatherd in a tent taking refuge from the hot sun.

Sounds of smacking, grunting, and brusque comments made Olaf realize they were interrupting the herder's midday meal. Olaf and Torgier peered inside and saw a squat, middle-aged man eating dates and *couscous.* He was licking his fingers and wiping the remains on the front of his *galabia.* Bits and crumbs from his meal clung to a few wiry whiskers that protruded from his plump cheeks.

"Excuse us, but we wish to see Yusef the goatherd. Do you know where we can find him?" Olaf tried to be as polite as he could.

The man grumbled something that Olaf and Torgier didn't understand, so they repeated themselves. Spit flew from his lips as he yelled impatiently, "What do you want with Yusef?"

"We want to do business with him," Olaf answered.

"What kind of business?" the goatherd asked curiously. He motioned them inside his tent. "Yusef does not make it a habit to do business with Vikings, but maybe I can help. What is it you are wishing to trade?"

"I want to purchase some slaves from him. Children, primarily, because they are small and can be useful on my ships. I am prepared to trade valuable goods for them," Olaf explained. There. He had cast his hook. Now he hoped the Bedouin would bite and give him the information he wanted.

"Yusef does not sell children. He is a very wealthy goatherd. How dare you insult such a great sheik. Now get out of my tent before I summon the market soldiers," the fat man seethed. Olaf gave it one last try.

"A sheik as great and powerful as Yusef does not become so merely by selling goats. You and I both know he sells children, and I need to buy some. If it is gold or dirhams you want, I have plenty to give you for your troubles." Olaf leaned right up to the man's face and hoped he convinced him.

Torgier reached around his neck and took off two large gold chains and laid them at the man's feet. Olaf saw the man drool as he snatched the gold from the tent floor quicker than a cat pouncing on a mouse. Immediately, the herdsman gave Olaf the information they needed.

Torgier and Olaf could hardly wait to tell the others. Yusef had left just hours earlier. He was headed for the Valley of Kings. The herdsman told them Yusef had plenty of children with him—from lands of the midnight sun. This convinced Olaf that his son and the others must be among them.

In a few hours it would be getting dark. Then they could leave for the Valley of Kings. They stocked up on water, food, and torches for traveling at night. Olaf even bartered for a few camels to hold all of their packs and supplies. What if the man had lied to him? What if Thor and the others were already dead?

At sundown the Viking party headed west for the Valley of Kings. Ben and David paid little attention to the landscape because there were no real landmarks out here. No pyramids, no monuments. Only lots of sand and rocky beige cliffs. They saw an occasional temple facade carved into a cliff, but that was it. No trees, no birds, no rivers, no rolling green hills. Endless sky and sand stretched for endless miles.

The Sahara Desert covers most parts of Northern Africa. By now, Ben and David felt as if they had traveled much of it. They were sick and tired of sand. There was sand in their shoes, capes, pants and shirts—even inside their underwear. It hurt to sit or lie down because sand had invaded every pore and crevice of their bodies—ears, nostrils, armpits, and more. When they shook their heads, sand flew out from their hair.

Although the boys decided they wouldn't be much interested in going to the beach for a long time, the thought of their lake cabin made them homesick. "I wonder if our folks are still looking for us," David murmured.

"I hope Mom isn't crying too much. If they found our bikes in the woods, they probably think we got kidnapped," Ben said.

"Do you think we'll ever get back?" David asked with tears filling his bloodshot eyes.

"I sure hope so. I can't wait to take a bath and wear something that doesn't have sand in it," Ben said. They stopped talking about home because it upset them. Instead, they just stared down at the never-ending sand and trudged onward. A dark grey-blue replaced the pinkish-beige color as twilight ended. Soon night and its nocturnal creatures would come.

Sleep during the day was difficult for our travelers as they brushed away scorpions, insects, lizards, and other creepy crawlers. After a couple days, the Vikings were well into the Valley of Kings. Olaf wondered if the fat old man in the tent told the truth about Yusef. He seethed at the possibility the man had taken his gold and given nothing of reliable value in return.

By dawn on the third day, they found shelter out of the hot dry winds at the base of a high sheer wall of rock. Someone suggested that from the mesa on top of the cliff they might be able to spot Yusef's caravan. Olaf and Torgier would wait until just after sunrise to climb to the top. Ben and David were assigned the dreaded task of checking crevices and small caves for rattlesnakes, scorpions, and other poisonous vermin. Since they were the youngest, they could do it or refuse. But refusal meant no food.

Shaded cracks and overhangs were perfect places for the despised creatures. The boys used their long walking staffs to probe into hidden areas and frighten off vermin. They tapped their sticks several times on the ground to stir a rattle from a dark hole. If they heard nothing, they thrust their sticks in to see what came out.

Just as Ben discovered a nest of scorpions and began furiously stomping on them, David screamed. A rattlesnake was poised ready to strike him. Ben left the scorpions and ran toward David to distract the snake. With two targets, the rattlesnake was confused. Ben began taunting the snake with his stick. David slowly picked up a large rock, never taking his eyes off the snake. He carefully raised the rock over his head. Smash! The rock hit the snake's head just before it could strike Ben. Both boys were trembling. Sidewinders were bad enough, but now they had to be aware of poisonous snakes, too.

They searched the immediate area and decided to call it quits. But they would sleep better knowing there were fewer scorpions and at least one less snake to crawl up their pant legs while they slept.

Olaf and Torgier began studying the cliff. Light was just making its mark on the dark blue sky. They discussed the best route and identified the safest handholds and footholds. It would be a hard climb. After a few faulty starts and falling rocks, the two were on their way up the face of the cliff. The men encouraged them from below. Olaf and Torgier refused to look down the sheer wall lest dizziness would paralyze them. An hour or so later, the two were at the top. As they heaved themselves over the edge of the cliff, Olaf and Torgier caught their breath and then gazed down over miles of sand dunes stretched before them.

During Olaf and Torgier's climb, Ben and David watched small rocks glance off the side of the cliff and bounce into a crevice at the base of the wall. Their necks ached from looking upward. They were bored. Ben picked up a pebble and threw it at David's back. David retaliated with a quick toss to Ben's chest. A small war ensued as they dove for cover behind boulders and peppered each other with small stones. This was fun. They were actually enjoying themselves for a change. The other Vikings stared at them in disgust for playing while lives were in danger and work was to be done. But Ben and David didn't care. They played their game and counted points for every direct hit.

While David frantically searched for more ammunition, Ben moved to another boulder closer to the rocky cliff. There was a dark area behind it, a hole into which pebbles from above had disappeared. Ben thought it was just a shadow, but as his eyes adjusted to the darkness, he noticed a cobweb drifting in a breeze. The cobweb covered a hole big enough for a man to crawl into. Ben threw a handful of pebbles into the hole to scare out any snakes. Silence. Then he heard a rain of pebbles hit. Ben lost interest in their game and called for David to come over.

"Is this a joke? Are you going to pepper me with pebbles when I get over there?" David was skeptical.

"Nope! Come here and look at this." Ben urged. David approached his older brother's turf with caution and a handful of stones. Then he saw what Ben was staring at.

"Throw your stones in there and let's listen for them to hit," Ben said. David tossed stones into the hole, and they counted the seconds until they heard the impact.

"One thousand one, one thousand—" they echoed. Over a full second. The bottom was at least twelve feet down. Maybe this was a cave they could explore.

Eagerly, Ben and David began to brush away stones and sand that had piled up near the hole. They uncovered a smooth surface people had placed there, so they kept sweeping with their hands and capes. In minutes, a form took shape in the sand. It was a floor made of smooth stones.

Meanwhile, Olaf and Torgier had spotted a large caravan heading directly west, deeper into the desert. From atop the mesa, they could see for miles using their telescopic tubes which cut down on glare from the sun. The tubes worked almost like modern sunglasses. Peering through their primitive telescopes, Olaf and Torgier watched a long dark blob move like a very slow centipede over the desert sand.

"That must be Yusef!" Olaf shouted. "It is the largest caravan we have seen. Those tiny brown dots have to be goats. They are too small to be camels."

They watched for several minutes to be sure they knew Yusef's direction wasn't going to change. They put their telescopes in their belts and began to plan their descent.

As Olaf peered over the ledge, he felt nauseated. It was a long way down and there was nothing to land on but solid rock. As Olaf looped his rope around a large boulder, all heads below turned toward new excitement on the ground. Torgier and Olaf stopped to gaze down at what was happening. Had someone been bitten by a snake or scorpion? "I'll bet that one of those foolish boys has been hurt," Olaf grumbled.

Torgier shouted for the Vikings to hold the bottom end of the rope. The rocky descent seemed a little less treacherous when Olaf and Torgier could look down on familiar faces. Torgier tested the rope with a few jerks and pulls. He tossed it to the ground in a gently uncoiling stream. The men below prepared to guide the rope and provide slack as the two descended.

Torgier hoisted himself over the side while grabbing the rope behind his back. With his right hand behind him and left hand in front, he placed his two feet firmly against the wall. Only his head was sticking above the mesa floor. Olaf bid him good luck.

"Take your time, Torgier. We have all day. Don't look down, and just concentrate on your footing," Olaf said.

The sun beat down on them and the heat reflected directly off the rock wall. Torgier was halfway down the cliff in about five minutes. His hands were sweating, and he was fighting panic. He inched over to a small ledge and sat for a few minutes to regain his strength and confidence. From his position, Torgier could see Ben, David, and a horde of men hunched over a bare spot and sweeping away sand. They labored like a bunch of worker ants. This sight took his mind off the descent.

Olaf shouted, "Should I toss you your sleeping mat and a jug of mead? Perhaps some fresh fruit." Torgier looked up and squinted at Olaf.

"I'm going. I was just watching our two small friends. It seems they have found something next to the cliff wall."

"They probably will be rewarded for their troubles with the stings of scorpions," Olaf shouted.

Torgier concentrated on the rest of his descent. Finally, his feet were on solid ground. It was Olaf's turn. He tested the rope and looked for tears or weak spots. He went over the side with no sign of fear. Torgier tended the rope's end.

Within ten minutes, Olaf was at the bottom, his arms limp from coming down the rope without resting. Several Vikings rushed over to tell the two climbers about Ben and David's discovery.

11

Underground Tomb

The men tugged at Olaf and Torgier and led them to the spot where David and Ben waited. They had found something that could be important. The crowd parted like the Red Sea to reveal two excited boys. Olaf and Torgier stepped onto a smooth stone floor with a large gaping hole where the floor met the cliff wall. In an attempt to widen the hole, the group had been chopping at the hole's edges with rocks. Ben and David shouted in unison, "Look closer. Look into the hole."

"Well, I'll be a Swedish mule!" Olaf gasped in astonishment. His eyes were round like full moons as he stared into the man-made abyss. "It's a stone staircase leading under the cliff."

"We went only as far as the stairs led, right up to a door in a wall. We think this might be an Egyptian tomb. Maybe it even has gold and jewels." Ben was breathless with excitement.

"If it does, we must agree to take only enough treasures to pay Yusef to get back our children. The gods must surely be with us, for you and your brother have brought us good fortune once more." Olaf spoke in a hushed voice.

Olaf, Torgier, and the others began removing rock from around the hole. In a few minutes the entire staircase was revealed. "There is something familiar about this scene," Ben whispered. They counted the stairs—sixteen. King Tut's tomb had sixteen steps to its outside entrance. Could they be at the entry of this famous pharaoh's tomb? After all, they were in the Valley of Kings where dozens of pharaohs were buried.

It could be just another empty tomb, ransacked by grave robbers centuries ago. On the other hand, it could be loaded with riches, completely undisturbed. Ben and David stared at each other. Their mouths hung open. Only in their wildest dreams would two Michigan boys enter a mummy's tomb.

Ben and David were demoted to the rear of the digging party. They crouched down to watch Olaf enter the outer door into a darkened hallway. The space was barely big enough for two people to squeeze through. The Vikings gathered around the entrance to the underground stairs.

"You're blocking our light. Clear a path so we can see ahead," Olaf shouted. They were reluctant to move. Nobody wanted to miss anything. They secretly hoped that Olaf would begin throwing out treasures of gold and silver to them as he foraged ahead like a gopher. Greed took over their common sense once again.

"What do you see?" Torgier asked as he handed Olaf a piece of burning firewood.

"There is nothing so far but dust and plain rock walls," Olaf responded. Quickly Torgier climbed in after him with another piece of burning firewood. "I think I have found something in this wall." Olaf's voice echoed, but it was a signal the men awaited. They fought to squeeze into the opening, but the hallway was narrow and had a low ceiling. Only a few men could join Olaf and Torgier. David and Ben hung back from the crowd hoping to get news of what was happening.

Clink! Clink! Clink! It was the sound of Olaf's ax against rock. Ben and David shoved their way through the men. "What did they find?" Ben asked breathlessly.

Torgier shouted, "We found a doorway hidden in the wall where the hallway ends."

Excitement grew outside the entrance as the men talked and whispered among themselves. The clinking of axes and wedges continued and soon handfuls of rock were being passed, hand to hand, up through the hole in the stone floor. It reminded Ben of a badger digging a den and tossing dirt behind him.

A slight breeze escaped from between stones as Olaf's fingers traced the cracks. Torgier held the burning sticks which offered only a flickering light. The tension mounted as the men pushed at a stone-sealed doorway. What would they find? Would there be images of horror and evil? Or, would there be riches they never knew existed? Maybe it would be one of the ancient Egyptians' tricks—just an empty room. Olaf continued chipping away at the wall. Finally he had chipped free a large enough chunk to be taken out and laid to the side.

Torgier helped Olaf lift away more large pieces of cut and fitted stone. On the count of three, they lifted each rock from shoulder level and threw it to the floor.

The others were paralyzed with fear. For better light, they had replaced the burning sticks with torches. Flames from the torches flickered in a breeze from some hidden source. The wind made an eery sound. Olaf and Torgier grabbed the torches and cautiously lifted them toward a new dark hole, shielding them from the wind.

When shouts of excitement echoed from the hole, the men pushed each other as they tried to get a better view. Olaf's torch had shown another hallway strewn with broken rocks and stones.

Olaf desperately wanted to push farther into the desert before they lost track of Yusef, but Ben convinced him that if he kept digging, they could find many rewards that would be useful.

So far, the boys' involvement had resulted in good fortune for Olaf and his men. There was the boys' discovery of the labyrinth's solution, the bailiff's chamber, safe passage from the castle, and the strange compass instruments they carried. Olaf decided to follow Ben's urgent hunch and discover what strange things would come from this hole in the ground.

The men preferred to work through the eery night because it was much cooler. Olaf, Torgier, and the others crowded into the hallway and into the second passage where they reached another apparent dead end. Olaf began to smash the wall with his hammer, thinking of the pagan god Thor's hammer as he did so.

They watched as Olaf enlarged a dark hole in the white plaster wall. Olaf turned to the boys and said in an irritated voice, "If this is just another rock-filled tunnel, we'll be heading out after Yusef as the sun sets tomorrow. If we haven't lost him already."

He gave the boys a disgusted look as though they were solely responsible for his every disappointment. They knew they would never regain Olaf's respect if this turned out to be a ransacked tomb. But Ben had a hunch it was King Tut's tomb. He hoped the tomb was still filled with riches.

Olaf smashed at the wall until there was a space big enough to squeeze through. Some were fearful of what lay beyond, but Olaf was too impatient to care. He thrust his torch through the new hole and waved it around so he could see what was in the room. Flames flickered as air from the passageway was sucked inward to fill the chamber's airless space. Olaf was grateful that it was not another flight of stairs or a rock-filled hall.

"I see some things along the wall in the back," he shouted as he peered into the hole.

Olaf dropped his torch and pushed himself through the opening. Yells echoed in the chamber beyond the hole. "We have struck gold. There are more riches here than in any castle or monastery we have plundered." Olaf was excited. Suddenly the men poured into the chamber. Olaf ordered them to calm down.

"Remember, we are here to gather just enough gold to buy back our children," Olaf shouted to the unruly group.

Ben and David pushed their way through the throngs of men lining the hallway and managed to get to the chamber door. The hole was now the size of a small doorway. Ben stared at the hieroglyphics over the doorway. "David, look! That's King Tut's name. A feather, water, half disks, a profile of a bird, an Egyptian cross, the staff, and a thing that looks like a tree. It all spells Tut-ankh-amen. And over there it says 'tomb.' There's a shape that looks like a T, a half disk, a comblike figure and a bent feather. Just what we thought. We've discovered Tut's tomb before it was robbed."

David was overwhelmed as he stared at the picture writing on the walls. Ben shook with excitement. He grabbed David and pulled him into the chamber. "We have more news to tell Olaf now that we know it's King Tut's tomb."

Olaf was feverishly looking for anything of gold or silver that could be carried easily. All around him lay baskets and pottery that he carelessly threw and broke in his greedy attempt to find treasure. Ben and David were horrified.

"This is just what the pictures of Tut's tomb looked like when Howard Carter found it. David, Olaf is the one who ransacked it so long ago," Ben whispered to his brother.

"And we're helping him do it?" David was ashamed.

"Is that all there is in this miserable tomb? All of this work for one tiny room in the bottom of a desert floor," Olaf yelled. All Olaf found or "chose" from the treasures were tiny gold statues of animals, half-men and half-god figures along with some trinkets. In his quest for handy treasure, Olaf failed to notice the gilded throne chairs, benches laced with gold and jewels, priceless couches, 4000-year-old burial wreaths and many other costly items too large to carry. In the mess he created was a tiny stash of things that Olaf decided to keep for himself.

"He's a wild man! Do you think we should tell him about the other two rooms?" David asked.

"Only if we can get him to agree not to destroy anything, but that's like asking a bull to be careful in a china shop."

Olaf picked up a huge rock and looked around the walls for a place to continue smashing. "Oh no! We've got to tell him before he destroys what's left," David said.

"Wait. Please do not destroy anything else. There are two secret doors here. The gods have spoken to me, Olaf. Listen to them. They have decided that if you destroy anything else, horrible deaths will come to you and all of your children," Ben shouted. "If you do not stop smashing stuff, none of your men will get the treasure you promised them.

Olaf calmed down. "Prove this, what you know from the gods. Where are those secret doors?"

"Only if you give your solemn vow to all of us not to destroy any more of the ancient king's treasures," Ben replied.

"I give my word. I will not ruin anything. I will take only whatever treasure we need to buy back our children," Olaf said.

David poked Ben, "Well, at least he's an honest thief."

Olaf yanked Ben by the arm and demanded that he show him the secret entrances. Ben stared at the wall opposite the hole they came through and pretended to be in a trance. Suddenly his arm pointed straight out. He crossed the room and stopped at the wall behind a gilded chair. Running his hands along the wall, Ben pretended that the gods had guided him to the spot.

Ben had read everything he could find in their mother's library about King Tut's tomb. He had seen pictures after Howard Carter excavated the treasures, so he knew where the doors were located. It was a great trick. Olaf and the Vikings would be very impressed.

Olaf commanded that Ben's directions be followed to the letter since he wanted no harm to come to his men or their children. Olaf stared with wide eyes at Ben. He was sure Ben was possessed by one of the main Norse gods: Odin, Thor, or maybe even Freyr.

Olaf sent for the ships' carpenters to unseal the tomb's first door. He wanted to make certain the gods were not angered. It took a while before the plaster seal around the door was chipped away. Olaf insisted that chunks of plaster be saved so they could add water to it and reseal the doors on their way out. Big sections of painted plaster were carefully removed and set aside. Little by little, the tiny door was exposed. Olaf was breathless as he waited for the carpenters to finish.

They discovered a small dark hole in the wall and Olaf dropped a torch inside. It was another room. But this one was smaller and contained numerous baskets, containers, and wooden boxes all piled up on one another. True to his word, Olaf lifted each lid and basket with great caution. He was disappointed, however, to find that the containers held foods, wine, clothes, and other everyday items that a king might need in the afterlife.

Ben had predicted there were two rooms. Olaf was still a believer—unless the next try failed. Ben hoped his memory about King Tut was on target.

Olaf and his helpers emerged from the dark cramped annex as carefully as moths from a cocoon. Finding nothing of value to use for future bartering, Olaf ordered the room sealed up. Another search began for the valuable treasure that Ben had convinced Olaf was in the tomb. The brothers saw how he treated the annex room, so they thought it was safe to tell him the location of the burial chamber door which led to the treasury.

Ben tapped lightly on the glass of his compass so the needle would stop spinning. David held the flashlight as they stood in the dimly lit antechamber. Flickering flames bounced off the walls and ceiling and played tricks on their eyes. Olaf peered between their heads. Mystified by the strange powers he thought Ben and David held, Olaf had learned after the annex episode not to question them.

"North is there," Ben wailed as he pointed to his right. He added a theatrical quiver to his voice as he continued. "Just about in the middle of the wall is another hidden doorway. There you will find King Tut's actual burial chamber." Ben and David continued to exude an aura of mystery and power as they revealed their "secret."

They refrained from telling Olaf what other facts they knew about Egyptian tombs. A pharaoh's burial chamber was always located at the north side of its tomb complex. Just before King Tut's time, the entrance had been moved from the exact north side of new tombs and pyramids to an off-north direction. That way thieves could not tunnel directly into the burial chamber, steal the treasures, and be on their way.

The boys remembered from Mom's books that the floor plan of Tut's tomb was almost an H-shape. So just east of the burial chamber should be the treasury chamber. Ben and David shook with excitement at the prospect of being among the first to discover King Tut's treasures.

Again, the men chipped away at the painted walls inside the dark room. It was hot. Furniture and artifacts were shoved aside to reveal a mural depicting the boy king's life. It showed scenes of boats floating on the Nile River. Happy people were eating good food and drinking wine. The gods were bestowing blessings of life and good crops. The mural also showed treasures of gold and jewels. The gods and people had on their best linen clothes, colorful earrings, bracelets, and necklaces which held pieces in the shape of animals.

Anubis, the god of afterlife, was shown greeting King Tut. He held a staff and whip, which were symbols of power used by Egyptian kings. Anubis had a dog face and a human body.

Near the center of the wall, between images of Anubis and King Tut, a tiny crack in the plaster was chipped away to reveal the left side of a doorway. Olaf nervously supervised the opening of the door to make sure the men were being careful not to cause too much damage to the wall. Torch in hand, he nagged the men about chipping too hard or going too fast or too slow. When Olaf's nagging became unbearable, the men ignored him and concentrated on removing large sections of the wall's mural.

This doorway was larger than the others. Olaf hoped that the room and treasures beyond were also larger. Ben and David became increasingly anxious as each piece of plaster was removed. They already knew what treasures lay behind the painted wall.

The men packed in behind Olaf and Torgier to see what lay ahead. They had to dig into yet another room, which was like a walled vault that had been placed inside—like a box within a box. But once inside, the shivering flames from the torches revealed the secrets of this room.

Gold gleamed everywhere. There were gold statues, gold chairs and couches. And there was King Tut's gold sarcophagus, a fancy coffin which held his mummified body. Such items could not be easily carried across the desert, however. So the men searched frantically through reed baskets and clay pots for smaller items of gold and jewels that could fit into their backpacks and pockets.

Ben knew what they had to do. The secret to such smaller treasures was hidden in King Tut's coffin. Carefully they lifted the lid of the first sarcophagus and then a second. When they finally managed to lift off the third lid, there was King Tut's mummy.

It lay in a gooey heap of tar and resin that was supposed to protect the king's remains. Ben had forgotten about that. It would take too long to cut and scrape through the hardened black mess. In the mummy's wrappings lay the boy king's necklaces, pins, bracelets, amulets and other accessories he would need in the afterlife. After telling Olaf where to find the other treasures, Ben and David felt they had done enough to help and kept the rest of Tut's secrets to themselves.

Ben and David heard the chinking of metal. Olaf was gathering jewelry he found in a small chest. He held some of the pieces up to the torchlight. Shimmering in the glow were gold necklaces, bracelets, and earrings. They were exactly like those painted on people in the mural outside this chamber.

The gold jewelry was inlaid with blue lapis, green jade, black onyx, and sparkling precious and semiprecious stones. Many were in the shape of Egyptian gods and animals. There was a serpent armband, a scarab pin for a cloak, earrings showing the Egyptian sun disk, and many other flawless pieces perfectly preserved by the dry desert air.

Olaf was overjoyed at their discovery. He held up each piece of jewelry as if he were the artisan examining his own work. All the pieces, except for two, he wrapped carefully in a piece of leather and placed in his knapsack. He turned to look at Ben and David who remained at the back of the crowd.

As an expression of his gratitude, Olaf held out two pieces of King Tut's accessories. To Ben, he gave the gold and lapis cuffs that the king's personal guards wore to protect their wrists. To David, he gave a gold, onyx, and jade belt. The boys didn't want to accept these priceless treasures because they were stolen goods, but Olaf was insistent. He did not want to anger the gods. Besides, the boys thought, getting the children back was the most important purpose of this adventure. And, maybe these items could help.

Ben and David were the envy of the other Vikings, who received nothing as yet from the tomb's treasures for all their hard work and patience. They knew the gold and jewels would be used to regain their most important treasure: their children—to bring their children back home. But Ben and David felt like young deer in a strange forest surrounded by a pack of drooling, snarling wolves who were about to attack. Olaf glared at the men to let them know they were to leave the boys and their reward alone.

With the excitement over, the tomb complex was sealed up. Everyone moved into the hot sun and waited for sunset before continuing their trek westward across the Sahara Desert. Could they find Yusef and the children before it was too late?

12

At Death's Door

The Vikings headed the direction Olaf and Torgier had seen Yusef's caravan travel. Olaf knew they were at least three days behind Yusef, but he hoped that Ben and David had some more "magic" that would help them catch up. Water was running low and the men were short tempered. They were not used to such intense heat day after day.

Something up ahead was flapping in the wind. It made a snapping noise like a flag on a pole, and the men rushed to the top of a sand dune to see what it was.

Olaf and Torgier slid down the dune's slippery slope. They found a battered old tent partially buried in sand, its poles still firmly planted. Olaf signaled the men to come and help unearth the huge tent.

The tent could accommodate several dozen people when its flaps were tied to the end poles. Olaf couldn't believe their luck and glanced suspiciously at Ben and David. He was sure they had something to do with it. This tent, however battered and torn, was a welcome sight to the weary Vikings. Their tent of sewn-together capes could now be dismantled and the capes returned to the men who had donated them.

As they sat under the tent's shade, Olaf looked around at his men. They couldn't go much farther without replenishing their dwindling supply of water and food. The bundles the camels carried were almost empty. Olaf sensed that his men needed more incentive to travel on. He was aware of the men's jealousy toward Ben and David and the gifts they received from Olaf's bounty taken from the tomb. He expected this could become a divisive problem. He got an idea.

"Whoever volunteers to scout ahead and find an oasis or a party with water and food will get these two gold statues," Olaf said. He reached into his bag and pulled out two solid gold statues of King Tut and dog-faced Anubis. Each was about a foot tall. All eyes widened as they viewed this treasure. The statues meant a great deal of wealth to the younger Vikings who did not have much of their own.

After a few seconds of staring and murmuring, Vikings began to assemble in pairs to volunteer. If the chosen pair were successful, each would have one statue—a very tempting offer.

Olaf chose Sven and Olin as scouts since they were the most physically fit, and they never complained. They were clearly pleased to be given the opportunity. Other Vikings offered extra food and water to the travelers. The pair carried four capes which had been left sewn together for shelter.

Some were clearly relieved that they were not the chosen ones, despite the promised rewards. Many Vikings had gotten sick from germ-ridden foods and lost weight. Some looked like modern prisoners of war. Their clothes were ragged and many had cut their leather boots down to make sandals. They wrapped the extra leather around their heads for sweat bands or shade from the piercing sun. Ben and David looked at the men and then at their own ragged clothing and beaten bodies. They wondered how much longer they could survive and whether Olaf was being realistic about this mission.

Olaf warned Sven and Olin before they left. "We will wait no more than four days for you to return. If you do return, you will be heroes. If you perish in the desert, you will be mourned by us for your courage and spirit in the face of danger. I will have a *skald* write a poem about you so that you will be part of history for your offsprings' honor. You will not be forgotten. Here is my *solarstein.* Take it so that you may find your way. May the gods be with you." And with that, the pair were off.

There were a couple hours of daylight left, so the *solarstein* would be useful, but by night Sven and Olin would rely on the stars to point the way. The weary group watched the scouts depart until they looked like tiny sand beetles on the horizon. Waves of heat rose from the desert sands and made the landscape look wavy. Everyone hoped and prayed that Sven and Olin would return safely.

Most of the men gathered under the ragged tent, but there was not enough room for everyone. The lower-ranked Vikings had to use the capes and unused clothing for shelter. The other Vikings had earned higher status by surviving numerous battles, showing courage, being generous with their plunder or, above all, proving loyalty to the group's survival.

Ben and David were pleased to be invited into the main tent where Olaf was sitting. But the smell was horrible. Despite the dry desert air, everyone had been sweating for days. They took off shirts and boots and rolled up their pants. The smell of dirty feet and sweaty bodies filled the air. Vikings were used to the odor, but it made Ben and David gag.

Bearded sunburned faces with exhausted eyes piercing below bushy eyebrows showed the men's hunger and fatigue. Ben and David, hungry and thirsty, became even more anxious when Olaf made an announcement.

"Everyone will have to turn in their bags of water and other drink. We will ration water to two swallows per person—morning and night. We must survive for the children's sake. We are Vikings and can endure any adversity to succeed at this most important mission."

Groans turned into shouts, and the boys thought there would be a mutiny. The men were already angry at not getting any tomb treasures. Now water rationing was forced on them. The men knew their abilities, but they also knew their limitations. And they were near the end of their rope.

Olaf waited for his men to stop shouting. The atmosphere was extremely tense. Olaf stood up.

"Men, you will be greatly rewarded when our mission is completed, and we are safely back in Norway. All of us suffer right now. A mutiny would not be in anyone's best interest. If I hear of anyone plotting against me, the penalty will be as it always is: death. It will not be quick and painless; it will be slow and painful. You will suffer much more by plotting against our mission than you will by working with us." As Olaf spoke, someone began collecting the water supply.

Ben and David looked at each other. Things were worse than they thought. They sat in the shade and waited for nightfall. With their shoulders hunched and fingers drawing patterns in the sand, they were silent and thought of home. It seemed like months had passed, but it had only been a few weeks.

"You think Grandpa rigged something in that metal detector before he gave it to us? You know, like a time machine. Maybe that's why he let us use it," David said.

"Why would he put us at risk like that? That's not like Grandpa. What a dumb thing to say," Ben replied.

"Maybe he wanted us to have a real life adventure. You know Grandpa. He thinks kids watch too much TV and waste too much time on video games."

"I don't know. Maybe this has nothing to do with his metal detector. Maybe," Ben paused, "maybe the dagger made it happen." He took a deep sigh. "I can't tell what's real and what's fantasy anymore. Maybe this is nothing more than a bad nightmare. I sure would like to go to the mall and have a Coke. I'd give anything to see some cars." The two boys sat with knees pulled up to their chests and resumed tracing in the sand. They imagined they were back in Michigan sitting on their own beach.

Suddenly, their thoughts were interrupted when the big tent's flaps started to snap fiercely. The top of the tent filled with air and bulged like a balloon and then came plummeting down on their heads. Wind blew from every direction, creating mini tornadoes. Plumes of sand lashed at them as the winds howled.

Nobody knew what was happening. Then they heard someone scream above the winds: "Sandstorm!" These storms could last for days. Ben groped for David without success. All he could do was sit tight and cover himself completely with his cape. He curled into a sitting position, put his hands over his head and held on tightly to his cape. It was hard to breathe, but without the cape he would be breathing sand.

David never knew how much sand could hurt. It felt like someone was scrubbing his skin with steel wool. He shouted to Ben but couldn't hear him above the roar of the winds and the tornado-like swirls of sand. Terrified, each brother hoped the other had not moved.

"Ouch!" David yelled. Someone had stepped on his fingers. There was sand in every crease of his body. His eyes were scratchy and watery, his teeth crunched when he bit down, and his ears and nose were full of sand. David tried desperately to get the sand out of his eyes. By a crack of light coming through the cape, he noticed pink smudges on his fingertips. His eyelids were actually bleeding from the sand.

What about the water supply? Had someone stowed it before the storm struck? What if the storm lasts for several days? They couldn't survive without water.

David was tempted to give into his misery. But he thought about how disappointed he'd be in himself if he *did* give up. He had faith that somehow they'd be back home soon. That faith helped him force despair from his mind and to concentrate instead on staying put and surviving. He felt around for his backpack. All he felt was sand.

David thought of his parents and grandfather. His mother had always said to him, "Remember to *think* when you are in a crisis. You can always panic later. Giving into panic can turn a crisis into a tragedy."

He had to think up a plan. He crawled around feeling for his backpack. Had someone picked up his water? He needed to find Ben so they could help each other. He touched something soft and leathery and pulled it underneath his cape. Ben's backpack! He must be close by. Keeping his toe on Ben's backpack, he pivoted around that area reaching as far as he could. He bumped his head into a tent pole.

He and Ben had just been sitting to the left of the pole, but which way was left? He lifted his cape in hopes of getting a glimpse of Ben, but it was useless. It was like looking through the windows in an automatic car wash. Finally, he felt a soft lump, and he tugged at some clothing.

"BEN!" David shouted as loud as he could. Someone lifted his cape. Soon Ben crawled under David's makeshift tent. Pushing the loose ends of cape underneath their feet and legs, they were able to create an air space free of the swirling sand. David had never been so glad to see his brother. Ben shouted into David's ear that the storm could last for a few hours or for days. Both backpacks still held their supply of water and food. It felt good to have each other *and* their supplies.

As the brothers huddled together, their thoughts turned to Sven and Olin. The scouts had no shelter beyond the tent, and they could be buried alive by the time the storm subsided. Ben and David prayed that the scouts would survive their quest.

The storm ended at dawn the next day. Sven and Olin, if they were still alive, had lost only one night of travel. The Vikings shook sand out of everything and stretched their legs. Then they sought a place to go to the bathroom. The camp resembled the awakening of a group of bears that had been in hibernation.

Some younger men outside the tent had been nearly buried alive. Sand had piled up to the waists and chests of several men. The others frantically dug them out. Together they unearthed the half-buried tent and struggled to resurrect it.

In a strange way, the sandstorm was a blessing because there was plenty of work to keep them all occupied for the next day or so. Water rationing had begun. Olaf didn't want the men to be idle. Idleness leads to thoughts of rebellion. He prayed the gods would send Olin and Sven back with good news.

The Vikings were weary, thirsty, discouraged, and haggard. They were too tired to eat and too hot to move. Smells and fears of death hung over the camp like a thick veil. Ben and David were afraid they may never make it back home to Michigan. Men groaned, others fainted, and all seemed hopeless.

Ben was the first to see them. He nudged David out of his heat-induced sleep and pointed to a ridge. There were two lone silhouettes dragging something behind them. At first Ben thought it was a mirage, but David was pointing at the same spot. Others murmured and stood, weakly pointing to the figures.

With hoarse, scratchy voices in need of water, the men welcomed and congratulated Sven and Olin. It had been four days. The exhausted pair were a sign of hope in desperate times.

The heroes were quickly ushered to the tent. On the ground they dumped sacks of melons, dates, coconuts, and figs. The men fought to touch the food to make sure they weren't dreaming. For the first time in days, the sound of hungry men chomping on food, followed by loud belching was heard instead of moans of suffering. Olaf took charge of the food stores and rationed what they would need until their next supply.

Great news from Olin and Sven: the oasis of El Rashda was less than a two-day's journey. Plenty of food, shady palm trees, and fresh water were there. It also had a *souq* where they could get the latest news about herders and other Bedouin groups.

Olin said they had watched in awe as the wind picked up the sand and began to move it like a great wall toward the southeast, where they had just come from. They thought the rains were coming because the sky was so dark. But as they studied the landscape, they soon realized the darkness was caused by sand and wind. They ran as far from it as they could. When they stopped for breath, they could see in the distance a dark speck on the endless beige landscape. They thought they could see something twinkling for just a second.

Olin and Sven reported that they decided to rest when the sun was setting. The next day they learned that the dark speck was the rich oasis called El Rashda. The twinkling was from a small lake reflecting the desert sunlight. It was fringed with coconut palm trees that waved in the breeze like tall slender giants.

Sven added that the best news was that Yusef was there. He was selling some of his goats and bartering for slaves. And the slaves were children. Olin and Sven thought they had recognized some of the children. They didn't want to get too close and risk being noticed. The pair had looked around Yusef's camp rather indifferently so they wouldn't look like spies. It was not heavily guarded.

Olaf was so relieved that he returned everyone's bags of water. They had fruits and coconuts that would supply their liquid requirements for awhile. Olaf gave Sven and Olin the gold statues as he had promised.

Olaf peered carefully through his spyglass at the oasis village. He could see the black silhouettes of coconut palms against the dark blue sky. They looked like giant mops stuck in the sand with their fringed strands waving in the hot breezes. Olaf handed the spyglass to Torgier, who put it in his backpack.

"Now is the time for Ben and David to go with Sven and Olin. They will find Yusef and leave the boys with him," Olaf said. "We cannot simply stroll into Yusef's camp and make a successful rescue. There are too many people there for that. It will be up to you boys now. We must trust the success of our mission to your powerful magic and your wits. Yusef won't suspect two young boys of such trickery." Olaf touched their shoulders. This time he did not shove the boys.

"Well, off with you now and may the gods be with you. Remember, boys, we will be following you. We will be hiding in the sand dunes and rocks nearby. So do not fear we have abandoned you."

As the four left, neither Ben nor David said what was on their minds: Were they about to spend the rest of their lives as...slaves?

13

Well-Disguised Plans

Ben and David savored the sights and sounds in the oasis. The voices, raucous shouts, jingling of money, and other noises of its *souq* were music to their ears.

Villagers stared at them with suspicion. Why were these fair-haired and fair-skinned Northerners so far inside Egypt? Their clothes were tattered and dirty. It was obvious they were not accustomed to desert life. Ben and David did not sense as much hostility from these locals, however, that they had seen in Cairo and Thebes. Some Bedouins were downright polite and even smiled at the boys.

Before they left for Yusef's camp, Ben, David, Sven, and Olin found the town's well and replenished their bags of water. The well was the lifeblood of the oasis. But it was less of a drinking well and more like a swimming pool. Tiled with colorful squares, it was a long rectangular pool with a fountain in the center. The fountain gushed gallons of cool artesian spring water over its sides and into the pool. The pool's flat low sides served as benches for weary travelers and idle gossipers. Around the base of the fountain, buckets hung on hooks for public use.

Women and girls were gathered at the "female side" of the pool to do laundry and collect water. Sounds of laughter and chatter indicated that the well was also a place for socializing. Animals joined their owners at the well to quench their thirst. Camels, goats, and Arabian horses were slurping the refreshing water with great sucking sounds.

Men and boys were in various states of undress opposite the female end of the well. They stood in the well to wash off layers of grime and desert sand. Ben and David joined them. Sven and Olin stood to the side shaking their heads. David finally dared to ask, "Why don't you two come and wash up? It sure would do our noses some good." Ben and David laughed.

Sven was adamant. "Bathing is bad for you. You wash all your defenses away with water, and you can become deathly sick. I would not tempt the spirits with such stupidity."

Ben and David stared in disbelief and continued washing. With disgusted looks on their faces, Sven and Olin waited impatiently for them to finish. The boys wanted the moment to last all day. They took off everything but their underwear and dumped buckets of water over their heads and let it run down their bodies. They scrubbed themselves as best they could without soap. Brown rivers of desert sand and sweat ran down their bodies and collected around their feet. They splashed each other and laughed. Never had water felt so good.

The boys shook their torn clothes and washed their rough linen shirts. They rinsed their hair and smoothed it down with bare hands, ready to trade almost anything for soap and shampoo. But they felt much better than before. They put on their cool wet shirts, which dried quickly in the sun.

Ben, David, and the two Vikings walked to a fruit vendor. They bought some figs, pomegranates, and yams. Sven and Olin were amazed by how quickly the seller figured how much they owed. Tenth-century Europeans knew nothing about the Arabs' invention of mathematical use of the zero. Sven and Olin were still counting on their fingers when the fruit dealer figured out how much they owed. He tapped his foot as he waited impatiently for his pay.

At another stand, chunks of lamb had been skewered and roasted with onions and were served with a yogurt sauce. Four mouths watered as the smell of spicy meat roasting and smoking filled the air. A vendor handed the long sticks of sizzling lamb and onions to the drooling, hungry quartet. Ben and David ate theirs so fast that they burned their fingers. The vendor laughed and said something in a language the boys didn't understand. They had never tasted anything so good. They washed it down with grapes and figs and cold water from the well. They drank until their stomachs bulged and sloshed when they moved.

As the sun's orange glow faded, they sat under some palm trees and watched the stars slowly dot the darkening sky. It was their last night of freedom. Tomorrow they would be traded to Yusef as child slaves.

Dawn broke on the desert horizon as sounds of slurping camels and bleating goats were heard throughout the oasis. Ben and David were so groggy from a good night's sleep that for a moment they forgot they were stranded in the tenth century with a group of dirty, smelly Vikings and Bedouins. But it didn't take long for reality to hit them.

After they finished breakfast, Sven and Olin gave Ben and David the two statues to bribe Yusef. The four set out for Yusef's goat camp. All of a sudden, Sven and Olin grabbed Ben and David by their arms and shoved them. As they neared the camp, they had to convince Yusef that the boys were slave-children. Their backpacks were hidden underneath their capes along with other items they would need to pull off the daring rescue.

Yusef's luxurious tent stood out like a rose among thorns. It was carpeted with Persian and Oriental rugs. Yusef treated honored guests to the best food and drink as rich business deals were made from his throne of pillows. It was obvious that Yusef camped here for only a few days to stock up on supplies and to trade in goats and slaves.

Sven, Olin, and the boys were led inside the tent to face Yusef. He sat like a roly-poly king upon his pillows and drank a cup of thick Arabian coffee. He made no attempt to get up or invite them to be seated. He seemed to be ignoring them. Finally, Ben and David were shoved roughly toward him, and Yusef laughed at Sven and Olin for bringing him such "weak, skinny whelps."

"What kind of work can such weaklings perform? Can they round up goats for twelve hours in the baking sun? Look at the size of their arms. They are mere saplings," Yusef shouted. "You expect me to buy them? You should pay *me* to take them off your hands." His guards and assistants made fun of the boys' looks. It was part of a bartering game to pay the lowest possible price.

The boys' faces burned with embarrassment. They hated being laughed at. They cringed at the thought of rounding up goats all day in the hot desert sun. Finally, after much haggling by both sides, Yusef paid a modest sum for Ben and David. So he had been bluffing when he had called them skinny and weak. Yusef was pleased to have two healthy children to replace a couple weaker slaves.

The brothers were shoved into a battered tent that held dozens of children from all over Europe and North Africa. Most in this tent were from northern Europe. They had blond hair and blue eyes, a combination for which Arab slave traders got paid the most. The tent was heavily guarded by men with machetes and daggers. These children between the ages of nine and fourteen wouldn't be running away anytime soon.

Ben and David shuffled their way among the children who were leaving to tend goats and do other chores. They quietly whispered Thor's name. The children stared, but said nothing. They were afraid the guards would beat them.

"You over there! Get in line with the older boys and feed the goats," a guard shouted to Ben and David.

Ben and David obeyed as guards pushed and scolded them for talking to other children. They were ordered to take goats to graze at the edge of the oasis. The boys were determined to get this over with as quickly as possible. Being a slave was by far the worst ordeal they have had to endure. They were being treated as things, not as human beings.

Under the guards' watchful eyes, a blond boy managed to make his way over to Ben and David. He kept his eyes downcast, yet he watched the guards as they moved among the children or lounged in the shade of a palm tree. The blond boy cleverly wrapped the end of his headdress over his mouth and tucked it around the other side of his face so he could talk to the brothers without his mouth movements being noticed. Ben and David pretended to herd goats with their long staffs while they listened to the young stranger.

"I am Thor, the one you asked about," the boy whispered cautiously. "What do you want with me?"

"Your father, Olaf, sent us here to help rescue you and the other village children." Ben nodded to his right. "He is not far from here. He and his men could be behind those rocks over there."

David wandered slowly away from Ben and Thor so they wouldn't attract attention. Ben glanced up in time to see one of Yusef's guards shade his eyes with a hand. He gazed for a while at Thor and Ben, but then decided he had seen nothing unusual. The guard leaned against the tree and continued eating dates from a pouch attached to his sash. He sat down, faced the open desert, and pretended to be alert. But his eyes were getting heavy. This gave Ben a chance to tell Thor their plans.

"What is my father's plan?" Thor tried to conceal his excitement behind the cloth covering his mouth. His haggard blue eyes suddenly sparkled with anticipation.

Ben replied, "We must wait until we move away from this oasis. Do you know when that will be?"

"I heard the guards say something about moving in a couple of days, but I could not tell you for certain."

"Then we will just have to wait. In the meantime, we must not risk telling any of the others why we are here. You must not talk to us," Ben said.

"But you still have not told me what the plan is," Thor muttered. He seemed wary now.

"There are several plans, but we will let you know which one works out and when the time is right. It is important that you do not come looking for us," Ben whispered while he looked at the herd of goats.

The three boys moved slowly among the goats. Thor carried on with a lighter step. It was the first good news he had heard in over a month. Tonight he would dream of his father's longships and snow falling gently on the sweet pine boughs around their home near Bergen. Perhaps dreaming was a luxury he could afford once again.

It was two days before Yusef could rouse his sluggish body to move from the comforts of the oasis. He emerged from his tent one morning with a stubble of gray and black whiskers and puffy eyes. He announced this was move-on-out day.

Barking orders to his servants and guards, Yusef was in a nasty mood. No one moved fast enough, answered quickly enough, or did anything right. Yusef moved slower than a snail uphill. It was a chaotic morning punctuated with Yusef's angry shouts and demands. Chests were packed and loaded onto camels and then several would be unloaded because Yusef wanted some minor item from one. That was nothing but a power play, of course, a way to remind everyone who was boss.

At last, the tents were carefully folded, wrapped, and packed onto the camels. Meanwhile, the slave-children had been ordered to gather belongings, pack trunks, and round up goats and camels. There was mass confusion as children were pushed, pulled, and shoved around as they tried to obey conflicting orders given by irritable people. Finally, the long caravan was on its way. The children were relieved.

Ben and David noticed that, while Yusef was a desert Bedouin and claimed to be Muslim, few in his camp prayed toward Mecca five times a day. Nor did Yusef shun alcoholic beverages. Indeed, he guzzled expensive wines with a desert thirst. Later, Thor told them that the only time Yusef went through the motions of being a faithful Muslim was when he had to please business guests who were real Muslims.

Pack camels led the train followed by Yusef high atop his shaded sedan chair. Then came the goatherds and servants. Last, came the slave-children on foot. While Yusef rested his plump bottom on a cushioned seat and popped grapes into his mouth, the weary children hurried along in the hot sun tending to straying goats as the caravan moved slowly onward. But, not far behind this column of animals and people that stretched out like a beaded necklace, Viking fathers and brothers were watching, waiting, and ready.

Olaf and Torgier paused for awhile so they would not be noticed by Yusef's scouts. "We give them only until the third night. Then we must make our move," Olaf announced to his men.

"Let us hope that Yusef can be persuaded by those two young boys," Torgier replied.

"You are too pessimistic, my friend. They will succeed. I have faith the gods will inspire and guide them," Olaf said.

Ben and David were absolutely exhausted by the end of the second day's march into the desert. The slave-children had not been given enough water or food for the journey. When the column halted, they dropped onto the sand and slept where they fell. Ben and David moved beyond frightened and tired into seething anger. It was the motivating energy they needed.

The time was right to see Yusef. A last minute check of plans and they were off. Ben and David did not need to tell Thor. It was obvious as they huddled together that tonight they would begin the attempted rescue.

Ben and David waited behind Yusef's tent until sounds of his wrath were replaced with sounds of his drinking and contented belching. A surprise attack on a contented enemy was always best, Olaf had told them. So the two of them hunched in their capes like shapeless lumps in the dark as they reviewed their plan for the hundredth time. Finally, Yusef dismissed the last of his servants. It was time!

Ben and David lifted a corner of Yusef's tent and crept inside. Yusef did not hear them. His head was beginning to nod on a pillow and faint sounds of snoring could be heard. Ben and David sat directly in front of him and laid out their bargaining tools. Then David poked Yusef in the arm and awakened him.

"What? What?" Yusef snorted. Heavy, droopy eyes opened as quickly as they could and tried to focus on the objects before him. "What are you doing in my tent? Get out you filthy street rats. How dare you invade the tent of a sheik," he growled through clenched teeth. He was about to strike the boys and summon his

guards, but David quickly thrust one of the statues in front of his face. The luster and shine of gold caught his greedy eye. He gazed at the beauty before him. Foot-high statues of King Tut and Anubis stood near his feet like toy soldiers.

"Where did slaves like yourselves get such things of beauty and price?" Yusef asked. He scowled as he eyed the gold statues and glared at the boys.

The brothers sat opposite Yusef on a lush carpet with their legs crossed. They kept the statues out of his reach. They were terrified. Who wouldn't be? Yusef could easily have them arrested or killed by his guards and then steal their gold. So Ben set the hook before Yusef had a chance to clear his sleep-fogged mind.

"You have the tastes and desires of a great sheik, but these are mere trinkets. There are items of greater value and beauty where these came from," Ben announced, hoping he said it the way Olaf had instructed him. They prayed that this would convince Yusef, this king of greed, to hold out for more treasures rather than have them killed.

Yusef stared at them through narrowed eyes. Ben and David tried to look confident. All they could do was tremble and wait for him to make the next move.

"What would make you part with your gold?" Yusef asked as he stroked his stubbled chin.

"We will give you these solid gold statues—and the secret of where to find much more— in return for the freedom of all your slave-children," Ben said. "Just these two statues are worth far more than you paid for the children, and you know it."

"Impossible! Your offer is an insult. What would I do without their labor? Who would tend my goats and set up my camp?" Yusef scratched his head. Ben knew he had little time to convince Yusef this was a good deal.

"Yusef, you are a wise man. Surely someone as great as you can see that these statues of solid gold are worth much more than a hundred slave-children. These statues came from the secret tomb of King Tut-ankh-amen. We have been there ourselves. With his tomb's treasures you could afford to pay much stronger men to work for you. You could pay so much that people would beg to work for the great Yusef."

Ben rattled off his exaggerated statement as quickly as he could, knowing he could soon lose his audience if he were not careful. To their surprise, Yusef stroked his chin and stared into the distance. David half-closed his eyes, expecting Yusef to summon his guards. Both boys sat erect expecting the wrenching grip of death to seize them by their shoulders.

"I will free the child slaves for these gold statues and the secret of where to find the other treasures of Tut's tomb," Yusef announced with hands on his knees. Ben and David looked at each other and discussed his counterproposal in hushed voices.

"Agreed. But we will pay you with these statues now and a detailed secret of other treasures when the children are freed... tomorrow morning," Ben said firmly. Yusef agreed and greedily snatched up the statues. He was grinning when the boys left.

As David and Ben returned to the campsite, something nagged at them. Could they count on Yusef to fall for their offer, as greedy as they were sure he was? David reminded Ben that they still had modern "magic" in their backpacks if worse came to worse. So the boys went to find Thor and the others.

Word spread throughout the entire camp of slave-children. No one could sleep. Excited whispers in each slave tent sounded like a swarm of locusts. They would be free at last. Or would they?

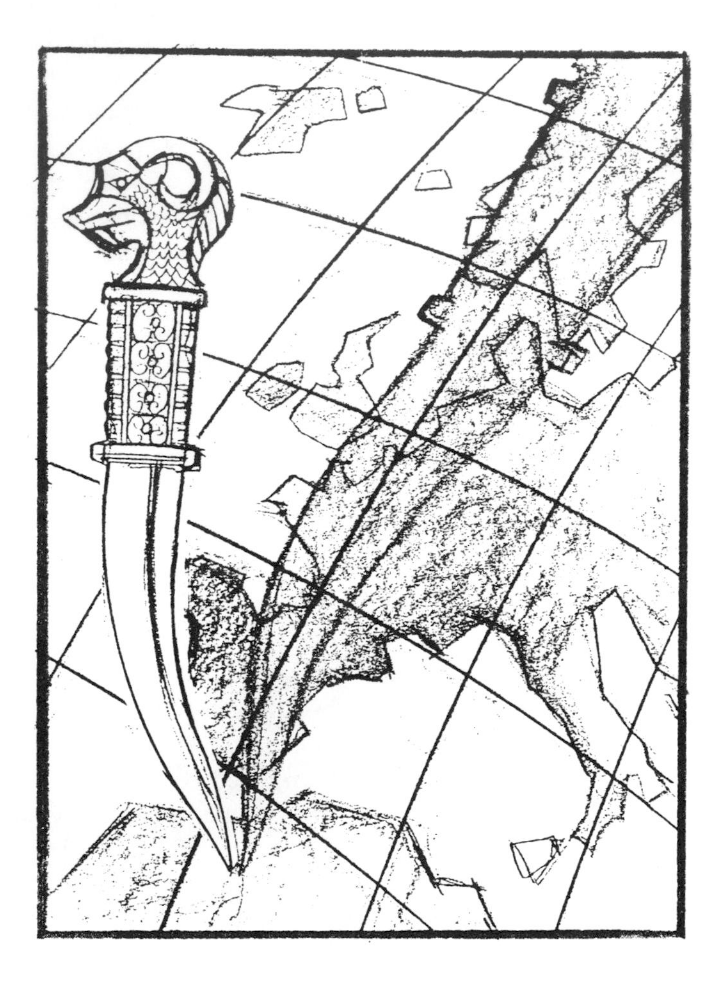

Drawing by Edgar Duncan, Jr.

14

Specter in the Night

"Get up, you lazy dogs!" The guards yelled as they kicked and lashed their whips at the children to get them ready for a day's work. What was happening? Had Yusef forgotten to tell the guards? Maybe he wasn't awake yet.

Suddenly, they saw the familiar potbellied figure emerge from his tent. Yusef yawned, stretched his stubby arms and scratched his face. He paid no attention to the guards or to dozens of screaming children.

Ben and David yelled, "We are supposed to be free. You promised us in return for the gold statues."

Yusef turned and bellowed an uproarious laugh. Then he pointed to them and joked with his guards that the two boys must be crazy. Ben and David fought a wave of panic. They both felt like a huge fist had just punched them in their stomachs.

"The gods will get you for this, Yusef. Tonight you will be visited by angry spirits of Pharaoh Tut-ankh-amen, because you have accepted statues from his tomb in bad faith and with a thief's spirit," Ben yelled.

Desert people were very superstitious, so he knew Yusef felt some fear even though he pretended not to care. Most Egyptians wouldn't even touch a Pharaoh's stolen treasures because they feared the "mummy's curse." That's one reason why thieves had to melt down ancient gold statues and jewelry into ordinary bars before anyone would buy them. Ben knew they had to take advantage of Yusef's fear.

The day seemed endless. Their spirits, which had soared just a few hours earlier, were poisoned with defeat and hopelessness. Thor avoided Ben and David like a contagious disease. The boys couldn't tell if the other slaves were looking at them with contempt or compassion. Ben wanted to tell them that there was a new plan, but he didn't want to give them false hope.

Ben and David prayed their modern "magic" would work. Under cover of darkness, three dark bundles moved as quickly as lizards on hot sand. A bright moon guided their movements around the slave camp. They scurried from one place to another to launch their scheme. Finally, the three dark forms were ready, and they merged as one.

At first, the main group of guards laughed at the tall dark shape standing before them. When did it appear there? How did it come to be standing a stone's throw from them? The light of their fires flickered and bounced off the tall black figure, making it appear even larger. Suddenly it backed up into the edge of darkness where the campfire's light couldn't reach. Intrigued, the men began to follow slowly, keeping their weapons ready should it prove dangerous. At the top of the tall figure, a face suddenly appeared that seemed to be illuminated from underneath. The men were no longer laughing. The face groaned.

"I am the spirit of Anubis, the god of the dead. There is one here who has accepted treasure from my world. Bring him to me at once, or all of you shall be rejected and tormented in my world of the dead." Ben's voice was amplified by his portable karioke.

The ghostly voice paused. "It is Yusef I seek. Bring this thief into my presence."

The guards were terrified, their eyes round like the full moon. Finally, the men retreated. Yusef was angry with his guards when they woke him from a drunken sleep. What was this nonsense they were jabbering about? He despised fear, especially in his own men. They refused his order to leave him alone. He threatened to have them killed. Still, they refused to obey his order. One guard released his sword from his belt.

"This spirit of the god of the dead is more powerful than you. If you refuse its order, all of us will suffer forever in Sheol."

Yusef angrily grabbed his robe and staggered into the darkness with his men. Swords were pointed at the tall dark figure whose face was, once again, not there. Yusef yelled. "It must be a prank from the little brats." He moved forward and the eery face was instantly illuminated. It moaned a horrible grizzly sound like an animal in great pain.

Finally, it spoke. "Yusef! I command you to release these children at once as you promised or the spirits of the Pharaohs will follow you and destroy everything you have. You will be cast into everlasting flames." The face disappeared again

"What are you talking about? I made no such promise," Yusef responded.

"You accepted stolen gold from Tut-ankh-amen's tomb in the form of two gold statues. You broke a promise and will be cursed by his mummy for the rest of your life."

The dark shape yelled in a weird voice. Ben had turned his karioke's volume knob so high that the sound was distorted. "I am the messenger of Anubis, here to seal your everlasting fate…and the fate of any fool who would protect you."

"This is crazy. Guards! I order you to capture that thing." But Yusef's guards did not move. Their swords were pointed at the dark figure, but their eyes turned to Yusef. Every guard knew the mummy's curse went back thousands of years and would fall on anyone who violated such a tomb or its belongings. The guards stood frozen in place, afraid to disobey Yusef. On the other hand, they certainly didn't want to inherit the mummy's curse.

Ben and David were encouraged. The old flashlight and karioke trick was working again. As Yusef yelled at his guards, Ben and David seized the opportunity to scare him once and for all.

Ben turned the flashlight on underneath his chin and spoke again in a loud, shaky voice, "Yusef, if you fail to believe my message, your men will know you are an infidel. So I will prove that my message is true. Behold," Ben's voice bellowed, "I will take this stick of wood and this rock and strike them together to create fire."

Rather theatrically, Ben held up a rock and a large wooden match and kept the red tip hidden between his finger and thumb. With a flick of his wrist, he struck the "wood" to the rock and sparks shot off into the darkness. Then, the flame. Murmurs of fear and amazement swept through the group as Ben held onto the burning match. He tossed it into the sand. While his guards were awestruck, Yusef needed more convincing.

David and Thor, still holding Ben on their shoulders, were getting tired and a bit shaky. David whispered to him, "Get your computer game out of your backpack. Maybe *that* will scare him."

Ben's arms disappeared underneath the cape. "You anger the spirits of the dead, Yusef," Ben bellowed. "Now they will speak to you, and I will translate for your guards."

His hands emerged from beneath the cape with a glowing blue square. He pushed a button. Noisy electronic sounds startled the guards. "Translation: Only an infidel will not believe our message."

The guards gasped. Several moved toward an open-mouthed Yusef. Ben pressed another button. Screeches, followed by a few bars of "Take Me Out to the Ball Game" sounded from the little box. "Translation: Infidels must die!"

Two more guards approached Yusef. "A magic trick," Yusef yelled. "Sorcery, pure and simple." His face turned from guard to guard. "It's all a trick!"

Ben turned up the volume and pointed the hand-held game towards his wary audience. He fiddled with all the buttons to make the ghostly figure of a baseball player appear on the screen. The box in the "spirit's" hand emitted high-pitched whistles, beeps, and short tunes.

Some of the guards got down on their knees and prayed. Others moved in closer, away from Yusef, curious about the talking figure. Ben was terrified they would find out what was going on. He whispered for David and Thor to move back into the darkness. Unsteadily, they walked backwards a few steps. The guards stopped, but now their swords were pointed at them, not Yusef.

"I will prove that my powers are from the afterlife. I will cover myself and point in any direction you call out to me without the aid of stars or sun," Ben shouted. He pulled the cloak over his head as David and Thor walked slowly in circles being careful not to drop him.

They stopped and someone shouted a direction. "El Quasar is to the northwest of here. Where is that?"

Underneath his cape, Ben used the low beam of his flashlight to look at his compass. Suddenly, his left arm shot out straight behind him. This time Yusef shouted, "El Kharga is southeast of here. Which direction is that?" Ben thrust his right arm out in front and a little to the right.

The murmuring in the crowd grew louder. How was the figure able to find direction so quickly in complete darkness? These were men of the desert whose survival depended on accurate directions. This was the most convincing demonstration. The tall dark being must be the spirit of Anubis.

Three more times Ben pointed out correct directions and that, along with a lot of angry moaning for effect, finally did the trick. Yusef, along with all the guards, dropped to their knees and asked forgiveness.

The spirit boomed in a loud voice, "Do not disobey me, Yusef, or all you touch will crumble to worthless sand. Stay where you are and release your slave children at once. Do not move from your position until the sun has fully risen, or your men must slay you and each other if they would escape the everlasting flames."

With that the spirit figure melted back into the darkness. Ben leapt off the sore shoulders of David and Thor. They ran to their tent to pack up their belongings and gather the slave children who were already waiting at the edge of camp.

Thor had ordered the children to fill their leather bags with water and take some food from Yusef's tents while they kept the men busy with their "magic" show. The children were terrified. They were waiting nervously under the protection of darkness, worried whether they actually would be freed.

With guidance from two flashlights, a hundred slave children poured into the vast desert. The night sky sparkled above them. When they were a safe distance, their cheers could be heard breaking the stillness of the night. The crowd of eager children walked through the desert sands to a large rock cliff topped by a mesa.

The charcoal sky began to fade to a deep purple as they neared the cliffs. Suddenly, dark lumps that they thought were rocks began to move towards them. Olaf, Torgier, and the other Vikings emerged.

Ben and David had never been so glad to see the rough, boisterous men. Olaf spotted his son, Thor, and rushed to embrace him. Other men recognized their loved ones and ran to gather them in their arms.

The brothers looked at each other wistfully. They wished that they, too, could be reunited with their parents. Ben and David stood as spectators watching the heartwarming reunion.

"Whoever would have figured that these so-called barbarians could feel this much emotion? I never imagined a Viking showing affection, did you?" Ben asked.

"No. I'd never believe it if I weren't here to see it," David said as he shook his head slowly. As the shouts subsided, Olaf approached Ben and David. They looked longingly into the crowd and felt, once more, the pangs of homesickness.

Olaf announced, "None of this would have been possible if it weren't for our real heroes, Ben and David. They have guided us and brought the spirits of good fortune to us on this journey. You have earned a place of honor among many great Vikings, and we will tell many sagas about you boys."

Olaf placed several chains of gold around their necks as he pronounced them true Vikings and immortal heroes, forever to be honored and remembered.

With that, the happy parents and children moved eastward to begin their journey back to Norway. But what would happen to Ben and David when they got back home—if they ever did?

Deep blue waves splashed salty foam over the bow and rolled across the wooden deck. Ben and David stood at the aft deck railing and were relieved that this adventure was coming to a close. They were assigned no duties aboard ship because of their hero status. The other children were given all the food and drink they could consume.

Olaf made sure all the children were comfortable for a long journey home. Room in the longships' pits was prepared for the children to sleep, eat, and regain their health. Many of them were sick, and all were fatigued from the hardships of slavery in the Sahara Desert.

Thor was glued to his father's side learning all he could about leadership and sailing. Olaf's face wore a beaming smile. Laughter and joy replaced the sounds of Viking bickering and short tempers they had brought into Egypt only a few weeks earlier.

During evening hours, the water was smooth. It looked like a mirror. In these rare moments the Viking men and children filled their time with games, storytelling, and singing.

Some Vikings even tried to teach Ben and David how to play *hnefatafl,* a board game similar to chess. The brothers caught on quickly since they already knew how to play chess. There were fewer carved pieces, only twenty-four, but the board and strategy were almost the same. Warlike strategies were used to defeat one's opponent while sharpening problem-solving skills and reasoning. Somehow they felt a strong personal tie to the game through moving the twelve Viking *jarl* and twelve warrior pieces. Playing *hnefatafl* was another reward they had earned for conquering a real enemy in the Egyptian desert.

The sky was dotted with clouds that looked like fluffy snowbanks. Their journey was almost over. There were several stops to disembark some kids who would go back home to France, England, and Scotland. The longships passed through the English Channel. Ben stared at his compass as he plotted the course in his mind. David peered over his shoulder.

Olaf smiled and said, "I have something to tell you two." Ben put the compass in his pocket, and they both turned to face the Viking with the fiery red hair. Olaf took out his jeweled golden dagger and sheath and held it out to them. "A gift to you, Ben, for all you have done. It was given to me by my good friend, Ahmed Ibn Fahad, a courageous Moroccan. I am in your debt forever. If you are ever in trouble, just ask for Olaf the Lucky."

Ben was astonished. He now held in his hand the same dagger he had that summer day in the woods of northern Michigan. Ben cradled it in his hands as he remembered what had happened when they had found it...so long ago.

Olaf turned to David and gave him dirham coins and another gold wrist protector. The boys replied with the customary courtesy their parents had taught them, but Olaf's gesture of thanks left them nearly speechless. This just wasn't like him.

Returning Olaf's generosity, Ben reached into his pocket and took out his compass. He pressed it into Olaf's palm and watched the red needle jiggle itself to north. "This should make your navigation much easier—day or night," Ben said.

Olaf looked at his gift with amazement. He had always liked it but had been afraid of its "magic." Olaf didn't question it now. He just gazed at the compass with its floating needle and told the boys about how lucky he and his Vikings were to have Ben and David with them on this life-or-death mission.

As Olaf left to show off his new navigating device, Ben fingered the dagger that now lay in his hands. It had a beautiful handle, a razor sharp blade, and fine weight and balance. It lay in his palms with perfect proportion between blade and handle. The sheath sparkled, casting colored shafts of light from its decorative gemstones. As he hefted the dagger, a strange energy coursed through his veins.

Ben remembered their struggle with Hammel's knights in the castle and thought of all the adventures he and David had shared with these Vikings. He peered at the ornate dagger and suddenly felt like brandishing it like a musketeer. He grabbed the scabbard with his left hand and pulled out the dagger with a flick of his right wrist.

As the blade slipped out from its protective covering, the seas began to pitch and roll as heavy swirls of wind and foam gathered around the ships. The sky was a stormy gray and the weather grew angry. The roar of the wind became deafening as if a great vacuum were sucking them in, and then suddenly, everything fell silent and dark.

But where were Ben and David?

15

Through a Time Warp Tunnel

"Ahhhh!" Ben and David screamed as they hurtled through layers of clouds. Lightning flashed around them. Dirhams shot by like bullets. Hammel's rickety old bailiff ran ahead of them. Dozens of belly dancers waved gold King Tut figurines at them. End over end, Ben and David hurled through the air. They passed through spirals of multicolored lights like something from a roller coaster ride. Only, all of it seemed so real. And the brothers knew it was...real.

Crunch! They landed on a bed of acorns and pine needles. "Ow! I feel like every bone in my body is broken," David moaned.

Ben was too shaken to voice his own pain and discomfort. They glanced at each other for reassurance and looked around. They were back by the huge oak tree—in Michigan.

It was the end of a beautiful summer day and the sun was low in the sky. Crickets and bullfrogs were beginning their nighttime serenades, and several adventurous bats were seeking an early insect dinner. Behind a wild raspberry bush were two trail bikes—one red and one blue. The metal detector and their digging tools were right where they had left them. But there was no hole in the ground and there was no sea chest.

They were back home! They jumped to their feet and cheered. Ben was still holding Olaf's dagger in his hand and David still had on his golden wrist protectors. "How long have we been gone, Michigan time?" Ben asked.

"I don't know," David said as he gazed around. "Everything seems to be about the same as we left it. Before we started digging, that is. Maybe it hasn't been long at all." Somehow, their Viking clothes had been replaced with their T-shirts and jeans.

Then they heard Grandpa call them. They ran for their trail bikes and raced toward his voice. "It's almost nine o'clock. You two are very late for dinner," Grandpa scolded. But he hugged them as they leapt off their bikes. "We were getting pretty worried about you two. You lose track of time?"

"I guess we did. Hey, aren't we going into town for cheeseburgers tonight?" Ben asked. He wanted to find out what day it was.

"No, we're doin' that Friday, remember? That's two days away. It's getting dark and your mom's worried about you," Grandpa answered. Ben and David were ecstatic. It was still Wednesday, the same day they had left.

Their mother met them in the driveway with a flashlight in her hands. She hugged them and was glad they weren't lost in the woods after all.

"You two surely are dirty. It looks like you haven't washed your hair in weeks. But you're probably hungry, so why don't we get you something to eat," she said. "You can take showers later. Dad has a bonfire and barbecue started down on the beach. He has been in the woods for hours looking for you. So has Grandpa."

Ben and David groaned at the thought of more sand. But once they smelled food, sand was no problem. Sitting on logs near the fire, they ate like they hadn't had real food in weeks. The fire snapped and sparkled, sending red hot ashes and tinder toward the starry sky.

Between bites of spicy barbecued ribs and buttery corn on the cob, Ben and David stared at the stars. They wondered if Olaf and the other Vikings were looking at the same timeless sight. Was Olaf using the new compass or was he still guiding his ships by his old *solarstein,* planets and stars? After a mouth-watering dessert of warm peach cobbler and vanilla ice cream, Ben and David went upstairs to take long, long hot showers.

Ben grabbed a towel from the bathroom and ran to their parents' room to use the sauna shower with the built-in bench. It had steam nozzles to make a sauna, and it was exactly what he longed for. It took three separate washings before his shampoo foamed up. He turned the nozzles on as hot as he could stand it and leaned back on the bench against the cold tile wall, sweating out the Sahara sand and grime and...memories.

David reached for a clean towel in the linen closet and started his own shower. He stood for several minutes under shower heads letting the steaming water pour over his exhausted body. He lathered bubble bath all over his skin and marveled how wonderful it felt to be clean again.

When the boys emerged from foggy bathrooms, there was a tiny river of sand in each shower. Ben watched the sand snake toward the drain and wondered whether the grains were from the Sahara or their Lake Michigan beach. They cherished their clean pajamas, and they couldn't wait to brush their teeth.

Once they were in their beds, Mom and Dad came upstairs for their nightly ritual of prayers, talk, and hugs. "Mom, as an archeologist and historian, do you believe in time-travel?" David asked. Ben shot him a warning glance that he had already said too much.

Mrs. Ryan looked at both boys with a wry smile. "How time really works is a mystery. Any true historian knows that. The past and future can be so powerful in our lives today. So, who can be sure about time travel?" She kissed each of her sons good night. "Is that why you two were gone so long today?" She picked up their clothes strewn on the floor. "Time-travel is one thing, boys. But you sure did bring a lot of sand in here with you. You brought half the beach up here."

She fingered some of the grains of sand. Strange. It didn't look or feel like sand from their beach. With that she said good night and headed downstairs.

Ben and David laughed at their mother's comment about the sand. If she only knew. They stretched out across the clean cool sheets and enjoyed the luxurious feeling of their own beds. Ben took a deep breath of the sweet pine air that was drifting in through the window next to his bed. It was so good to be back home!

Late morning sunlight streamed in a sharp angle over his bed and nightstand. Ben opened his eyes and looked around the room. He tried to clear his mind. Then he remembered something important. Ben felt under the mattress for his dagger. He took it out to look at it just to be sure. "Nope! It wasn't a dream after all."

He remembered their adventure. A smile crossed his face, and he returned the dagger to his secret hiding place. Ben stared at the ceiling reliving it all and wondered how it could have happened. He looked at David who was still sleeping. He swung his feet over the side of the bed and tiptoed across the wooden floor.

His legs and back ached from yesterday's reentry onto a lumpy cushion of acorns and pine needles. Ben leaned on the windowsill, chin in his hands. He and David never slept this late, but they were worn out from their "trip." As he stared out the window toward the woods, he wondered whether they should tell anyone about their amazing adventure.

David yawned and rubbed his face as he shuffled to the window. Their adventure's full effect had not hit either of them yet. "There's Grandpa," David said. On the driveway below them, Grandpa was stooped over some hand tools. There was much clanking and banging of metal. Their grandfather turned to glance up at them. He was holding the metal detector, and its parts were strewn everywhere. He held up one hunk of metal and shouted, "I'll never get this thing put together again. I could make a time machine with all these parts."

Then, with a wink and a smile, Grandpa headed for his workroom. Ben and David stood speechless at their window, wide-eyed, as this beloved but mischievous old man lumbered off with a certain purpose about him.

GLOSSARY

Chapter 1

ancient—p. 1: very old, about two thousand years or more ago
crude—p. 4: rough, not carefully made
dirham—p. 5: Arabic silver coin that Vikings also traded and collected
runes—p. 7: Viking alphabet used in writing
Viking—p. 7: a Scandinavian warrior who often raided and plundered in other countries; from the verb VIK, which means "to raid"

Chapter 2

surly—p. 12: rude, short tempered
grettir—p. 13: large main house where a Viking chief lived with his family; it also was a social gathering place for the village
jarl (YARL) p. 13: Viking chief; usually got his position through excellence in combat leadership and sharing plunder generously
pallet—p. 13: narrow sleeping cot of hides or cloths attached to a wall
vague—p. 13: unclear, not obvious
mead—p. 14: a fermented beverage made from honey
serf—p.15: the lowest category in feudalism; by contract, a lord got exclusive use of a serf's work

Chapter 3

longship—p. 17: the Vikings' shallow-draft boats used for long sea travels and raiding
dinghy—p. 18: small boat used to transport people to and from ships
knorr—p. 19: Viking merchant ship used for importing/exporting goods
fjord—p. 20: deep inlets cut into mountains by earthquakes or glaciers

Chapter 4

keep—p. 26: a castle's main tower for the laird, his family, and important rooms
parapet—p. 26: walkways on top of a castle wall for guards to keep watch over anyone trying to approach a castle
peasant—p. 26: person who farms as a small landowner or laborer
portcullis—p. 28: a heavy wooden or iron gate at the main entrance to a castle; at the end of a drawbridge
barbican—p. 28: an outer guardhouse before the drawbridge
chief porter—p. 29: a guard who decides if you can enter a castle

gatehouse—p. 29: guards' room where the winch to lift the portcullis was located; a place to view activity at the main entrance

Chapter 5

entourage—p. 30: group of people assisting or attending someone
murder holes—p. 30: in ceilings over castle entrances; for dumping stuff such as boiling oil or sharp rocks on invaders
bailey—p. 30: the castle's central courtyard
bailiff—p. 31: an accountant who kept track of castle income and expenses; for security reasons, his office was hard to find
stealthy—p. 32: sneaky, undetected movement
projectiles—p. 33: targeted flying objects such as arrows
flailing—p. 34: beating back and forth
winch—p. 34: a handle that turns a rope or cable onto a spool.
laird—p. 36: a local Scottish lord or nobleman

Chapter 6

labyrinth—p. 39: a network or maze of passages and walkways
chasm—p. 42: a deep pit or opening
sconce—p. 40: a wall bracket to hold candles or torches
abyss—p. 44: a very deep pit

Chapter 7

warlock—p. 48: a male witch
chalice—p. 48: a cup used in communion to hold the wine
postern—p. 50: gated entrance at the rear of a castle

Chapter 8

camouflage—p. 51: disguise enabling a thing to blend into background
starboard—p. 52: the right-hand side of a ship (when looking out over the front or bow); the left hand side is called "port"
solarstein—p. 53: a crystal rock used by Vikings for locating the sun or bright stars in the clouds to plot a sailing course
opaque—p. 53: something you can't see through
Thor—p. 53: one of three main Norse pagan gods, Thor was in charge of the sky, thunder, lightning, and storms. The other two are: Odin, god of war and wisdom, and Freyr, god of agriculture and fertility
scabbard—p. 54: a case that holds a knife or dagger
souq—p. 57: an outdoor market in many Middle East countries
mesmerized—p. 57: awestruck, spellbound

galabia—p. 58: long pullover cotton shirts usually worn with long loose pants; used by Arabian men
chador—p. 58: long black robe worn by some Muslim women; it covers them from head to toe
bilge—p. 62: water that has leaked into a boat's hull or bottom deck

Chapter 9

tributary—p. 63: a stream that flows into another one making it larger
weigh(ed)—p. 64: to lower an anchor into the water; "aweigh" means to pull the anchor back up
smorgasbord—p. 64: an assortment of foods on a table from which people select what to eat
junk—p. 65: a Chinese boat; some were large but awkward
thobe—p. 68: a long cotton robe worn by Arabian men
laban—p. 69: a rich sweet drink made from goat's milk

Chapter 10

couscous—p. 76: Mediterranean dish made of tiny pasta pieces
sheik—p. 77: chief or head man of an Arab village or tribe
nocturnal—p. 78: animals that hunt or feed at night
mesa—p. 79: a high flat-topped hill
vermin—p. 79: small creatures such as mice, rats, creepy-crawlers

Chapter 11

hieroglyphics—p. 87: instead of letters, symbols or designs were used for messages, stories, or histories
sarcophagus—p. 91, a fancy decorated coffin concealing a mummy
amulets—p. 92: good luck charms worn on one's arms or wrists; pagans thought they could ward off evil spirits
scarab—p. 92: a carved image of a beetle; usually on stone or bone

Chapter 12

skald—p. 97: a medieval Scandinavian poet or saga writer
plunder—p. 97: treasures stolen on raids; kept as personal property
plumes—p. 99: a feathery puff of stuff such as dust, sand, or smoke
mirage—p. 101: a hot desert illusion, something seen that is not real
haggard—p. 101: a look of total exhaustion and weariness

Chapter 13

machete—p. 108: a curved broad-bladed sword used for chopping or hacking underbrush sedan chair—p. 111: a large comfortable chair enclosed by a covering on a framework of wood poles; used to carry someone wealthy

Chapter 14

specter—p. 117: a ghostly image

contempt–p. 118: scorn, dislike, lack of respect

Sheol—p. 119: in Hebrew and some Arabic dialects it names the underworld, where spirits of the dead go

infidel—p. 120: an unbeliever, a person who has no "proper" religious faith; the term's best known usage is by Muslims

sorcery—p. 121: bad tricks or hurtful magic

saga—p. 123: a long story telling of deeds and events in Viking history; usually mixes fact with lots of imagination and meanings

aft—p. 123: from "after," meaning behind or toward the back of a ship

hnefatafl—p. 124: a Viking board game similar to chess

disembark—p. 124: to leave a ship and go ashore

Chapter 15

serenade—p. 127: melodic song for an audience

sauna—p. 129: a steam bath created by pouring water on heated rocks; in northern European and Russian countries the bather often rolls in snow afterwards

ADDITIONAL SOURCES

Davidson, H.R. Ellis. *Viking and Norse Mythology,* 1996, Barnes and Noble, New York.

LaFay, Howard. *The Vikings,* 1972, National Geographic Society.

Magnusson, Magnus. *Vikings!,* 1980, Elsvier-Dutton Publishing Company, New York, NY.

Morley, Jacqueline. *How Would You Survive As a Viking?* 1995, F. Watts Publishing, New York, NY.

Simons, Gerald. *Barbarian Europe,* 1968, Time-Life Books, New York, NY.

Simpson, Jacqueline. *Everyday Life in the Viking Age,* 1967, Dorset Press.

Simpson, Jacqueline. *The Viking World,* 1980, St. Martin's Press, NY, NY.

SUGGESTED ACTIVITIES

1. Write a letter to someone pretending you are a Viking. Explain your activities and plans. To make the letter look really old, tear pieces off around the edges and dip in tea. Flatten to dry.
2. Using craft sticks and glue, make a model either of a Viking longship or a knorr. Don't forget the colorful sails.
3. Make up your own board game about Ben and David's adventures.
4. Illustrate your favorite scene in the story.
5. Draw a cartoon strip to explain a scene or event in the story.
6. What job would a Viking have today? Sailor? Navigator? Military officer? What kind of business would he or she own? Draw and write out an advertisement for a modern-day Viking occupation for the yellow pages.
7. Design your own Viking shield or piece of jewelry. Remember that they liked intricate swirling patterns with heads of animals (snakes were a favorite), dragons, and birds. They were fond of the colors black, blue, red, and yellow.
8. Similes (using "like" or "as") and metaphors compare two things. (Example: The boy moved as quick as lightning) How many similes or metaphors can you find and list from the story?
9. While remembering that it's usually not fair to judge people from long ago by modern standards, discuss questions such as these:
   (a) How were Olaf's Vikings different from today's gangs?
   (b) Was it okay for them to take stuff from Hammel's treasury and Tut's tomb?